A Halloween Surprise!

* * *

Decision made!

"I am *so happy* right now," Bella told Alfie. "I mean, I knew it was a really good idea. And I guess I could do it alone. But it'll be a lot more fun with you doing it, too."

"We gotta keep it a secret, though," Alfie warned her. "Because it'll be a hundred times cuter if we surprise everyone next Friday, right? And if it's a secret, no one can copy us."

"I can keep a secret," Bella said, crossing her heart.

"Me too," Alfie said, crossing hers. "So, what are we waiting for? Let's draw bunnies!"

"Bunnies," Bella agreed, selecting another marker and sniffing it.

"And then we can eat hamburgers," Alfie added as her tummy growled again.

"And afterwards, my mom can measure you for your bunny costume," Bella said.

Alfie smiled. "This is fun," she said. "Thanks for inviting me, Bella!"

Books by Sally Warner

✳ ✳ ✳

THE ABSOLUTELY ALFIE SERIES

Absolutely Alfie and the Furry Purry Secret

Absolutely Alfie and the First Week Friends

Absolutely Alfie and the Worst Best Sleepover

Absolutely Alfie and the Princess Wars

THE ELLRAY JAKES SERIES

EllRay Jakes Is Not a Chicken!

EllRay Jakes Is a Rock Star!

EllRay Jakes Walks the Plank!

EllRay Jakes the Dragon Slayer!

EllRay Jakes and the Beanstalk

EllRay Jakes Is Magic!

EllRay Jakes Rocks the Holidays!

EllRay Jakes the Recess King!

EllRay Jakes Stands Tall!

THE EMMA SERIES

Only Emma

Not-So-Weird Emma

Super Emma

Best Friend Emma

Excellent Emma

ABSOLUTELY Alfie

• and •

THE PRINCESS WARS

SALLY WARNER

illustrated by **SHEARRY MALONE**

PUFFIN BOOKS

PUFFIN BOOKS
An imprint of Penguin Random House LLC
375 Hudson Street
New York, New York 10014

Published simultaneously in the United States of America by Viking and Puffin Books,
imprints of Penguin Random House LLC, 2018

Text copyright © 2018 by Sally Warner
Illustrations copyright © 2018 by Shearry Malone

LIBRARY OF CONGRESS CATALOGING-IN-PUBLICATION DATA IS AVAILABLE

Puffin Books ISBN 9781101999974

Printed in the United States of America

Book design by Nancy Brennan

3   5   7   9   10   8   6   4   2

To Patrick Love II, who knows what
it's like to have a sister!
—S.W.

For Luke. —S.M.

* * *

Contents

{1} Ready for Some Fun! 1

{2} The All-Star Girls......... 10

{3} A Halloween Plan.......... 17

{4} Counting by Two 23

{5} Funny Bunnies............. 30

{6} The Same as Everyone Else .. 37

{7} Another Squabble? 42

{8} Taking Sides 48

{9} The Princess Wars 55

{10} Alfie's Idea. 62

{11} Please?. 72

{12} Secret 80

{13} Almost Heart-to-Heart 85

{14} Alfie and EllRay 96

{15} Feeling Guilty 105

{16} A Big Fuzzy Blur 113

{17} One Last Battle 120

{18} What You Do 127

Ready for Some Fun!

"EllRay needs some chili pepper flakes on his pizza," seven-year-old Alfie Jakes said at the dinner table. It was a cool Sunday night in the middle of October.

Perfect teasing weather, in Alfie's opinion.

"I do not," EllRay said, guarding his pizza with a skinny brown arm. "And you should talk, Alfie. At least I've got more than just bare cheese on my pizza. You *chicken*."

"Uh-uh-uh," their mom said from across the table, her finger in the air. "No name-calling, EllRay. You're eleven years old. You know better than that."

"He does know better," her husband agreed,

nodding. "And those pepper flakes are for your mother and me, Miss Alfie," he added. He helped himself to another slice of the medium "Cheese and Spinach Special" pizza he and his wife were sharing, and he gave it a good sprinkle of the spicy red flakes.

EllRay had Pizza Frank's "Meat Lover's Dream," and Alfie had "Just Cheese, Please." Cheese was Alfie's favorite food.

The Jakes family was hungry following their afternoon bike ride outside Oak Glen, an inland town halfway between San Diego and Los Angeles, California. Built partway up the side of a low mountain, Oak Glen lay sprawled across that mountain's rocky foothills like a sleeping cat, Mrs. Jakes sometimes liked to say.

She wrote books for ladies about the olden days, so she described things in a special way. That's what Alfie thought, at least.

Dr. Jakes was a geology professor at a university in San Diego. That's where the "doctor" in his name came from. He had driven the whole family—plus bikes, helmets, and plenty of water and snacks—outside town for their bike ride today.

They had unloaded their dad's old Jeep in a quiet area where scattered California live oaks grew on gentle slopes covered with dry brown brush and feathery weeds. Southern California's annual rainy season had not yet begun.

"We'll start here so we don't use up all our energy just getting out of town, like last time," Dr. Jakes had said, straightening his helmet.

On their bike ride two weeks earlier, the Jakes family had started at home—and only made it as far as the 7-Eleven on San Vicente Road before giving up.

"You took us all the way out to Witch Creek Road today, Dad," EllRay said at dinner, remembering the day's ride as he continued to protect his pizza from Alfie and the small jar of red pepper flakes. "I heard about that place before. Creepy," he added, fake-shivering as he gave his little sister a look that he clearly hoped would scare her.

"But witches absolutely aren't real," Alfie said, pausing mid-bite. "Are they, Dad?"

"No," he told her, patting his mouth with a napkin. "They are not real."

"People used to believe in them, though," Alfie's mother said.

"An early prospector might have thought some rocks or mountain ridges looked like a witch's profile, or maybe like a pointy hat," Dr. Jakes said. "That's probably how the road got its name, Cricket," he added to Alfie. "The Triassic Period," he added, thinking aloud. "Which means that area is more than two hundred million years old," he reminded the kids.

"And that means *dinosaurs*," EllRay said, smiling big.

"Early ones, anyway," his dad agreed, nodding.

"Oh, right," Alfie said, thinking she was being teased. "Dinosaurs. Where I was riding my pretty pink bike today, with the fancy tassels on the handlebars." Her bottom was still sore from sitting for so long.

"Let's get back to that witch thing for a second," EllRay said. "Because you know what? It's almost Halloween!"

"*Duh*," Alfie scoffed, shaking her head. "Like you and Marco haven't been planning for it since last summer."

"But we still haven't decided on our costumes yet," EllRay reminded her. "Because you never know what movies are gonna be showing at the last minute," he explained to his parents. "Some really cool character might come along."

"Well, now's the time to decide what you're going to be," his mother said, laughing. "Because you've only got about two more weeks, and if you're going to want me to help with the costume—"

"That's okay," EllRay said. "I want to make my costume myself this year."

Her big brother was really good at inventing stuff, Alfie thought, proud in advance.

But what was *she* going to be on Halloween? There were five or six costume ideas Alfie had been daydreaming about, depending on which of her second-grade friends she'd been playing with that day.

What Alfie wanted most of all was to fit in with all the other second-grade girls—because lately, she had started to feel that she was getting things just a little bit wrong.

For example, after Lulu Marino slept over one Friday night, she'd been surprised when Alfie said her mom was going to take them to the farmers market the next morning. "But why do you guys buy dirty vegetables in the high school parking lot when they sell nice clean ones at the super-market?" Lulu had asked, wrinkling her nose.

Was shopping at the farmers market a weird thing to do? And how many girls had Lulu told about it?

Then there was "Cute Barrette Day" just two weeks ago, Alfie thought, frowning as she remembered the second-grade girls' invention. She had plenty of cute barrettes. That wasn't the problem. But the other girls could easily change their bar-rettes around during the day, their hair was so floppy and loose. Alfie's mom had already fixed her hair for the day, though, and Alfie couldn't change it just like that.

And she had wanted to match—*exactly*.

"I remember when I was your age, EllRay," Dr. Jakes said, smiling again. "I couldn't decide between being a Teenage Mutant Ninja Turtle or the Terminator."

"They had Ninja Turtles when you were a kid?" EllRay asked, amazed.

"Thanks, buddy," his dad said, making a face. "That's when the whole thing started! It was a movie back then."

"Let me see," Mrs. Jakes said, also remembering. "When I was nine years old I wanted to be Catwoman, because she was a really amazing movie character that year."

"I remember," her husband said, nodding in an encouraging way. It was as if he thought his wife might be deciding that this was the perfect year to make her old dream come true.

She could be a kitty this year, Alfie was telling herself, adding another costume possibility to her list. Not like Catwoman, but a kitty like Princess, *her* kitty. The most beautiful cat in the world.

Alfie's mom sighed. "Well, my mother didn't think Catwoman was a proper costume choice for a girl my age," she said. "So I ended up being Marge Simpson."

"But, Mom," Alfie said, trying to picture it. "Marge Simpson is white!"

"Actually, she's bright yellow," her mother pointed out. "But we skipped the skin color and just went with the tall blue hair and the pearls. I was a little disappointed about the whole Catwoman thing, though," she admitted.

"I'm disappointed now, just thinking about it," her husband joked.

"I wonder if we're going to have the parade again at school this year," Alfie said, looking at her brother. She and sixth-grader EllRay were both students at Oak Glen Primary School. This was his last year there.

"Probably," her mother said. "But I haven't looked at the online calendar lately, I confess. I've been too busy with my book."

"And Halloween's on a Tuesday this year," EllRay reminded everyone. "Tuesdays and Wednesdays are the real dud-days for Halloween, too," he added gloomily.

"Oh, I think people will still manage to have fun," Dr. Jakes predicted.

Alfie tried to cross her fingers under the table. She was really ready for some fun!

"Speaking of fun," EllRay said with a grin, looking at his sister, "are you ready to lose big tonight?"

On Sunday nights, Alfie and EllRay played board games together. Their mom made them a special snack they were allowed to eat upstairs.

"What are we playing?" Alfie asked.

"I was thinking we could play that candy game," EllRay said. "Because of Halloween."

"Okay-y-y," Alfie said slowly, as if already planning her first move. "But I'm the one who's gonna win."

"Good luck with that," her brother replied.

2

The All-Star Girls

"We're here," Hanni Sobel said as her mom pulled up in front of Oak Glen Primary School the next morning. Alfie and Hanni were neighbors, and Mrs. Sobel and Alfie's mom shared carpool duty.

"You don't have to say that every single time, Hanni," Alfie said. "It's not like I don't have eyeballs in my head."

But Hanni could be kind of a know-it-all, Alfie reminded herself. A girl who liked to be the first one to announce things.

Hanni frowned, and her dimples disappeared. "I was just *saying*," she muttered, sounding sulky as Alfie waved goodbye to Mrs. Sobel's departing car.

"Hello, Miss Jakes and Miss Sobel," Principal

James called out from his spot halfway up the school's wide front steps. He took pride in greeting each student by name, EllRay had told Alfie the day she started kindergarten.

"Hi-*eee*," Alfie and Hanni chorused, waggling their fingers in his direction.

"You copied me, Alfie," Hanni said, raising her voice a little as they entered the school's crowded hall. "I invented 'Hi-*eee*.'"

"I'm not sure you can invent a word that everyone already uses," Alfie said carefully, not wanting to rile her sometimes-prickly friend—but not wanting to be bossed around, either.

Being in second grade felt a little like walking on a balance beam, Alfie had begun to think. The girls in her class were friends most of the time, but there were moments—like this one—when that could change in a flash.

"That would be like me saying I invented the word 'school,'" Alfie continued. "And then yelling at people whenever they used it."

"It's not the *word*," Hanni said. "It's the way I say it that's so cute."

Wow, Alfie thought, biting her lip. What was

up with Hanni today? They had been on-again, off-again friends since late last summer. Mostly on-again. Maybe Hanni had "gotten up on the wrong side of the bed" this morning—the way Mrs. Sobel sometimes said she did.

That expression meant Hanni woke up in a bad mood, Alfie had learned. But Alfie didn't believe in bad moods. A bad mood just meant you were being grouchy for no reason, in her opinion.

"Alfie!" Arletty Jackson said, bouncing up to Alfie and Hanni as they made their way outside. They were heading toward the picnic tables where the second-grade girls liked to hang out before class. "Did you finish your sentences? Our homework?" Arletty asked.

Weekend homework—what little of it there was—was Alfie's least-favorite part of being one of Mr. Havens's "All-Stars," his class's name for the year.

But Alfie relaxed, hearing Arletty's voice. They had known each other since preschool. And they were the only two girls with brown skin in Mr. Havens's class, not counting three girls who were more caramel-colored than brown, and who—so far—mostly hung out together.

Also, Arletty was easy to be around because she wasn't as much of an "uproar girl" as Hanni was, as Alfie's mom sometimes put it. A little peace and quiet—another of Mrs. Jakes's favorite expressions—was looking like a good thing today, with Hanni acting so weird.

"That homework was easy," Hanni said, jumping headfirst into the conversation. "All you had to do was to use capital letters right, Arletty. And punctuation marks."

"I know. I was just asking," Arletty said, sneaking Alfie a look. Her hands fiddled with the beads she wore at the end of her soft black braids.

Arletty was really fun and nice, all the girls agreed. So why was Hanni being such a pain?

"Like, two of my sentences went, 'My name is Hanni! I have a cat named Domino!' Capital H, capital D. Exclamation mark," Hanni continued in a voice loud enough for all the girls to hear.

Such as bossy Suzette Monahan, who sat at Alfie's table in class.

And always-cute Lulu Marino with her perfectly straight bangs, whose mother called her "my special darling."

And funny Phoebe Miller, with her swingy blond hair.

And husky-voiced Bella Babcock, their class's newest arrival, who had slowly gotten used to everyone in class—but who also didn't mind being on her own, or so it seemed to Alfie.

Alfie liked every girl at the table.

The All-Star girls were pretty cool, in her opinion.

The six other girls in their class were probably off playing somewhere, Alfie guessed—but they were nice, too.

"Stop showing off," Lulu told Hanni in a jokey voice. "Exclamation mark!"

"Don't tell me what to do," Hanni said—even though she sometimes tried to kiss up to Lulu. Not today, though.

"I think the buzzer's about to sound," Bella told Alfie. Bella looked as if she were thinking, *Please, please, please buzz, buzzer.*

"Nobody asked you," Hanni said without even looking at her.

Whoa.

Rude.

A few of the girls looked at each other, blinking like startled owls, not quite knowing what to do.

It was only Monday! School hadn't even started yet!

Yeesh.

"Come on, Bella," Alfie said, touching the girl's arm. "Let's be the first ones in class today. Arletty, you can come with us if you want. Mr. Havens will be amazed."

"Go ahead and run away," Hanni called after them. "Bye-*eee!*"

"Don't pay any attention to her," Alfie whispered to Bella. "Hanni's just being grouchy today, that's all."

"For no reason, probably," Arletty chimed in.

"But it's still gonna be a really fun week," Alfie told the girls, hoping it was true.

A Halloween Plan

"Listen up and settle down, All-Stars," Mr. Havens said after he had taken Monday morning attendance. He probably called out names like a San Diego Navy guy taking roll call, Scooter Davis told the kids at Alfie's table once.

Mr. Havens had set up five tables in his classroom this year, with five kids at each table. A few single desks were scattered at the back of the room, in case someone needed to work alone.

Their teacher was tall and strong, Alfie thought, admiring him. His prickly hair seemed to sparkle on his head, it was so short. He was always neatly dressed, complete with a skinny tie, lately. But he sometimes seemed to be bursting out of his shirt, his muscles bulged so much. He rolled his shirtsleeves back from his big wrists as if he couldn't possibly button them.

Mr. Havens had played basketball in college, and he coached the Oak Glen kids at recess, if they were interested.

EllRay loved basketball. He called Mr. Havens "Coach."

"Shhh," Scooter told the kids at Alfie's table. "He's talking."

Scooter's real name was Stephen, Alfie knew. The other three kids at their table were Arletty, Hanni, and Alan Lewis, another new kid this year. Alan's big thing was that he hated being called on in class, Alfie knew, and he was always worrying it was about to happen. "Is he looking?" Alan sometimes whispered, shrinking in his chair.

By now, the middle of October, Alfie and the other girls were getting used to having what they still secretly called "a boy teacher."

The boys in class had liked the idea from the very first day, of course.

"Oak Glen finally has a firm Halloween plan," Mr. Havens said, getting everyone's attention. "Principal James and the Parents' Association decided to move our annual costume parade to a week from this Friday, for those students who want to take part. But costumes are not required, of course. The parade will take place after lunch. Then everyone will return to their classroom for a class party," he added. "Nothing too fancy, just some juice and muffins, maybe. A few of our very generous parents will take care of that."

A buzz of excitement seemed to zip through the class.

From across the room, Bryan Martinez's hand inched up in the air, and Mr. Havens called on him. "But, Coach," Bryan said. "That's not Halloween. Because my mom said Halloween is on a Tuesday this year."

Alfie nodded in agreement, hearing this.

"It's 'Mr. Havens' when we're inside, Bry," his teacher reminded him. "And your mother is right. But it was decided that our celebration should be on a Friday afternoon, so it will interfere less with schoolwork. The whole week might be lost if we held the parade and party on a Tuesday."

This made no sense to Alfie. But—a parade! And a party!

Was she about to argue with Mr. Havens about the details?

No way!

"But, *Mr. Havens*," Suzette said, raising her hand, too, but speaking before he'd even called on her. "Does that mean that on the real Halloween, we have to wear *regular clothes* to school? And not our really cute costumes? Because I heard that wearing the exact right costume on Halloween can bring a person good luck for the whole year! And I'm gonna need it."

"Where in the world did you get that idea?" Mr. Havens said, laughing. "Wear the right costume on Friday, Suzette, and you should be okay."

Suzette looked as if her teacher had just taken away a present.

Alfie held her breath. Was Suzette telling the truth about the good luck, or was she making stuff up again? Suzette had vowed for one whole year that she'd seen the tooth fairy in person, for instance. And that probably wasn't true.

"You can wear your costume at home on the real Halloween, of course," Mr. Havens reminded

Suzette—and anyone else still listening. "If you go trick-or-treating, that is—or to some neighborhood party. However you celebrate this grand occasion. Maybe you can find your good luck then, if Friday afternoon doesn't work out for you." He smoothed his skinny tie straight.

"*Boo-o-o*," Suzette whispered under her breath.

Across from Alfie, Hanni looked disappointed, too. "No fair," she murmured, shaking her head.

"Be quiet, Hanni, or you'll wreck it for everyone," Scooter whispered, unable to help himself.

Alfie cringed, waiting for Mr. Havens to react.

"Would you ladies prefer to skip the Friday parade and class party altogether, and see how lucky you feel then?" Mr. Havens asked, folding his muscle-y arms across his chest and raising one eyebrow as he scowled in Suzette's direction, and then at Hanni. "Because that can be arranged," he said.

"No, sir," Suzette said.

"I guess not," Hanni said.

"You *know* not," Scooter told her.

"Scooter," Mr. Havens warned. "Now, All-

Stars. Let's get going with our Shared Reading, okay? Because I found a couple of really good books for you. Books that fit right in with both the holiday and the season, which is called 'autumn,' or 'fall,' by the way. Not that we get much of that here in Southern California. But I think you're going to like them."

And Alfie settled back in her chair for one of her favorite times of the day.

Counting by Two

"Oh, beautiful Princess," Alfie whispered to her kitten three nights later, on Thursday. She and Princess were alone in Alfie's room.

Alfie's homework was done.

Dinner was finished, the dishes had been rinsed and stacked in the dishwasher, and Alfie had already taken her shower.

This time was all hers.

"You're such a good kitty," Alfie told Princess, stroking her kitten's gray-and-white fur. "What do you want to be for Halloween, little girl? Hmm?"

Maybe at least one of them would come up with an idea.

Princess was almost four months old. She was

looking and acting like a small version of a cat now, and not a helpless kitten.

Springing into action, Princess grabbed a plush gray dolphin from among the other stuffed animals leaning against Alfie's pillows. The kitten starting kicking the dolphin hard with her hind feet. It was a real attack. "Princess," Alfie scolded, trying to rescue the beloved dolphin.

"Yes-s-s?" answered a high voice from behind the door to her room—which then swung open.

It was EllRay, pretending to be the princess Alfie had been talking to. He held out a cell phone—their mom's—in a pretend-dainty way. "It's for you, little villager," he said, adjusting an invisible tiara with his free hand. "Come on," he added in his normal voice. "Mom says you can talk for ten minutes, and then bring her phone back downstairs." He shook the cell phone a little so that Alfie would take it.

"But who is it?" Alfie asked.

"How should I know?" EllRay said. "I am D-O-N-E. Done, yo," he added, tossing Alfie the phone.

"Hello?" Alfie asked, feeling shy as EllRay

vanished back into the hallway, and Princess scampered to the top of her tower. "Hello?" Alfie said again, wondering if this was one of EllRay's tricks.

She'd been pranked before, and she *hated* it.

"It's me. Bella," a husky voice said.

"*School* Bella?" Alfie asked, because they had never talked together on the phone before.

"Uh-huh," Bella said. "Why? Do you know a lot of other Bellas, too?"

"Maybe I do, and maybe I don't," Alfie teased, trying to settle into the rhythm of the phone call as if she got them every day of the week—which she did not.

Was this what being a teenager felt like?

Cool!

"Um, well, I was wondering something," Bella said.

"Wondering what?" Alfie asked, hoping Bella would ask her about their math homework, "Skip Counting by Two." She had gotten it correct right away—for once.

Two, four, six, eight.

"Like, wondering-if-you-want-to-come-over-for-a-playdate-this-Saturday," Bella said, tumbling the words together in her hurry to get them out fast. "Saturday," she said again. "The day after tomorrow. But it's okay if you say no. My mom asked your mom, though, and your mom said I should go ahead and ask you."

"I know when Saturday is," Alfie said, trying to joke and sort out this unexpected information at the same time.

A playdate with Bella!

It sounded good. In fact, Alfie had been wanting to invite Bella over to *her* house sometime soon. Playing alone with one other girl was the most fun, Alfie thought. That's when you really got to know someone.

Bella Babcock's family had moved to Oak Glen a month after school started, so she was the last All-Star to enroll in Mr. Havens's class. Bella was an only child, and really cute, Alfie thought, with a few pale freckles scattered across her turned-up nose. Her short, tufty, dark-blond hair seemed to catch the sunlight like a magnet when they were playing outside.

Seeing how shy Bella was at first, Alfie had

volunteered to show her around Oak Glen Primary School. And she'd stuck up for Bella last month, when Lulu was mean to her for no reason.

Not that Bella needed to have someone stick up for her anymore, Alfie had seen over the past few weeks. Lulu apologized to Bella ages ago, which was a good thing, since she and Bella sat next to each other at the table behind Alfie's. And Bella had slowly but surely found her own comfortable place among the twelve other All-Star girls.

She fit in, but she also didn't seem to mind

going her own way. For instance, Bella had ig-nored Cute Barrette Day altogether—and it wasn't because she had short hair, either. Alfie had seen Bella wear cute barrettes in her hair before.

Bella just hadn't been into it that day.

Alfie secretly admired that.

"Well?" Bella asked. "Do you wanna come over Saturday or not?"

"What time?" Alfie asked.

"Your mom said she'd drop you off after you guys finish at the farmers market," Bella told Alfie. "It's okay if you say no," she said again, sounding uncertain for the first time.

"Of course I'm not saying no," Alfie said, her cheeks hot at the mention of the farmers market. "I wanna come over for sure. Are you kidding me? It'll be fun!"

"Yeah," Bella agreed, and Alfie could almost see her relieved smile. "Maybe we'll even make some cookies, or bounce on our trampoline," Bella said. "Or *both*. But I'm going to stop talking now, because my mom wants her phone back. Okay?"

"Okay, sure," Alfie said. "My mom wants hers back, too."

She'd been wondering how to hang up right, when they were done—without having the other person end up telling the other girls, *"She hung up on me!"*

"So, goodbye," Bella said. "Press the red phone button so it's over, Alfie."

"You first," Alfie said, smiling. "Because you called *me*."

"Okay," Bella said—and *poof*!

She was gone.

Funny Bunnies

"Hi-*eee*. Here are some apples," Alfie said to Bella on Saturday morning at the Babcocks' front door. She felt shy as she thrust the bulging recycled bag from the farmers market in Bella's direction. "My mom says they're a special kind," she added, sounding doubtful—because how special could apples be? There were green ones, sour, and red ones, sweet.

Period.

And apples were a weird present to bring to someone, in Alfie's opinion.

But Alfie's mom was still watching from the car, so there was no way Alfie could ditch the apples in the bushes. Mrs. Jakes tooted the car horn once, waved, then pulled away from the curb. The two moms were going to have coffee together later on, when Mrs. Babcock drove Alfie back home.

"Thanks, Alfie," Bella said, handing the apples to her mother, who had just appeared in the front hall.

"*Alfie*," Bella's mother said, after she'd sniffed the apples and smiled in appreciation. "That's such a cute name, isn't it?"

"I guess so," Alfie said, frowning. "It's short for 'Alfleta,'" she explained, feeling even more shy than before. "It means 'beautiful elf' in this olden-days language my mom knows about from the books she writes."

"Oh!" Mrs. Babcock said, surprised. "I didn't know your mother was a writer."

"Uh-huh," Alfie said, nodding. "My big brother EllRay has a weird name, too," she explained, wanting to get it over with. "'EllRay' is short for 'Lancelot Raymond,' or 'L. Ray.' EllRay. See?"

"He's in the sixth grade," Bella told her mom, her eyes wide. "He likes basketball. But we gotta go play now, Mom. Okay?"

"Of course," Mrs. Babcock said, laughing. "I'll be around if you girls need anything. And lunch is later on. Hamburgers," she added in a tempting voice.

Alfie was ready for a hamburger *now*, she thought, her stomach gurgling as she followed Bella to her room. But she guessed she could wait.

Bella's house was pretty cool—although there were some moving boxes that hadn't been unpacked yet in a spare bedroom the girls passed. "We have too much stuff for the house this time," Bella said, following Alfie's gaze.

"This time," Alfie repeated to herself, curious.

Bella's room was cute. She had a pretend zebra-skin rug—pink and white striped—that Alfie *loved.*

"Wanna draw pictures?" Bella asked. Now *she* was the one who sounded shy.

"Sure," Alfie said, still looking around the room. "What of?"

"Our Halloween costumes, maybe," Bella suggested. "The parade's next Friday. And the party."

"Oh, right," Alfie said, settling down on the zebra rug with the pad of newsprint and the markers Bella handed her. "What were you thinking of being, Bella? Because I don't know whether to be a bumblebee—my neighbor's old costume, except the stinger is broken—or a kitty. Or a teenager, like our babysitter, Bree. Bree's really cute. And she wears tons more makeup than my mom, so dressing up like her would be fun."

But would being a bumblebee or a kitty or a teenage babysitter bring her good luck for the rest of the year? Alfie couldn't figure out how.

"Huh," Bella said, examining a scented marker. "Good ideas. Do you think Mr. Havens is gonna wear a costume to school?"

"Probably just a funny hat or something," Alfie

predicted, thinking about it. "Unless Mrs. Coach gets him to wear something cute."

"Mrs. Coach" was what the All-Stars secretly called Mr. Havens's wife, who had not yet been seen by any of the second-grade kids.

Scooter said his mom sometimes called Mrs. Coach "the unicorn," in fact, as if she might be imaginary.

"I don't think Mr. Havens would ever wear anything *too* cute," Bella said, laughing.

"Me either," Alfie said. "But what are you gonna be, Bella?" she asked, reaching for a black marker—for the bumblebee stripes.

Bella leaned forward, excited. "I'll be the cutest bunny ever, I think," she said. "See, my mom found some really soft fleece at the store," she explained. "And she said she could get some silky stuff for the insides of the bunny ears, and make a perfect fluffy tail, too. She's really good at sewing."

Bella paused. She looked as if she had something else to say.

"What?" Alfie asked.

"Well, we could be two funny bunnies *together*, that's what," Bella told her. "If you want to be one, that is. It's just an idea," she added.

"But my mom can't sew anything right now," Alfie said. "She's writing another book, and she has to finish it on time. It's like extreme homework."

"My mom could make the costume *for* you," Bella said, sounding excited. "She said she would. If you want to be a bunny, too, I mean," she added, backing off a little.

"That *might* be okay," Alfie said, trying to imagine it.

The two funny bunnies. Bunnies were rabbits, right? And rabbits were definitely good luck. Or their feet were, anyway, Alfie thought, trying to remember the details of that goofy old story.

Two bunnies, or *rabbits*, meant eight rabbits' feet, Alfie figured, secretly doing the math on her fingers. Unless their front feet were called paws, she corrected herself silently. But even *four* rabbits' feet were enough to bring two girls good luck for the year, for sure! It was easy math.

"You're thinking about it," Bella said, excited.

"I'm thinking *yes*," Alfie said. "If your mom really wants to make both costumes, I mean.

Because—you're right. It would be cute. And lucky, too," she added, nodding.

Decision made!

"I am *so happy* right now," Bella told Alfie. "I mean, I knew it was a really good idea. And I guess I could do it alone. But it'll be a lot more fun with you doing it, too."

"We gotta keep it a secret, though," Alfie warned her. "Because it'll be a hundred times cuter if we surprise everyone next Friday, right? And if it's a secret, no one can copy us."

"I can keep a secret," Bella said, crossing her heart.

"Me too," Alfie said, crossing hers. "So, what are we waiting for? Let's draw bunnies!"

"Bunnies," Bella agreed, selecting another marker and sniffing it.

"And then we can eat hamburgers," Alfie added as her tummy growled again.

"And afterwards, my mom can measure you for your bunny costume," Bella said.

Alfie smiled. "This is fun," she said. "Thanks for inviting me, Bella!"

The Same as
Everyone Else

"I don't like it when we have to do journal entries for weekend homework," Hanni said two days later. It was another Monday morning, and she and Alfie were on their way to school in the Sobels' car. Hanni kept her voice low, even though her mom was listening to the news on the radio as she drove.

"I know. I don't like it either," Alfie said. "Weekends are when we should be doing stuff, not writing about it. But at least we only had to write four sentences—about the toys we like to play with when we're inside. 'Something About Me,' Mr. Havens called it."

"Yeah," Hanni said. "But with punctuation

and capital letters. And a beginning and an end. And on top of all that, Mr. Havens will probably make us read them out loud."

"Only some of them," Alfie reminded Hanni. "Mr. Havens is pretty nice about journal entries. He says that the rule is, we can keep our journals private if we want. We get to raise our hand and volunteer if we feel like reading something out loud."

This was the rule Alan Lewis liked best, of course, Alfie thought, thinking of the shy boy at her table. Alan would probably never raise his hand in class—all year long.

Everything was private with him.

"Mr. Havens might change his mind some day about the volunteering part, though," Hanni pointed out. "And he gets to read *everything*, whether we raise our hand or not," she added, fluffing her wavy brown hair in a way meant to show how irritated she was. Hanni's hair was still a little wet—from the shower, Alfie guessed, smelling shampoo.

"But Mr. Havens *has* to read everything, because he's the teacher," Alfie said. She gazed out the car window at the houses they passed as she half listened to what Hanni was saying. What kind of private stuff was Hanni writing, she wondered? All *she* had written was about playing with Princess, doing the old wooden jigsaw puzzles her mom had played with when she was little, and collecting stickers. Especially the puffy kind.

She could not imagine Mr. Havens being too interested in any of that.

Now, if Scooter Davis wrote about playing with matches in his spare time, or if Bryan Martinez wrote about secretly skateboarding down the stairs inside his house, that might get Mr. Havens's attention.

"So I just made stuff up for my weekend homework," Hanni whispered, as if she were giving Alfie the solution to some pesky problem.

"Really?" Alfie asked, her eyes wide.

"That way," Hanni said, "no one can make fun of me if I accidentally write something weird."

She and Hanni were different in almost every way, Alfie thought. But basically, what Hanni just said proved that different people could want the exact same thing. In this case, to fit in.

"But kids don't make fun of you," she told Hanni, staring at her neighbor with wide brown eyes.

"They might start," Hanni said. "Remember that time when Phoebe read aloud from her journal? When she said she was afraid of ladybugs—because of their houses being on fire in that nursery rhyme?"

"She really got teased," Alfie said, nodding.

And Hanni had been one of the kids doing the teasing, she thought.

"The boys scared her, too," Hanni said. "They kept pretending to throw ladybugs on her—for two whole weeks."

Until Mr. Havens had put a stop to it, Alfie remembered.

She bit her lower lip. Were her classmates going to tease and laugh at her about how she liked to play with her mom's old wooden puzzles? Did *that* sound weird?

"We're here," Hanni said as usual when they pulled up in front of Oak Glen Primary School. She turned to glare at Alfie as if daring her to complain that she'd said it again.

But Alfie didn't utter a word.

Another Squabble?

"You *guys*," Suzette said at one of the second-grade girls' picnic tables a few minutes later. "Let's all figure out what we're going to be on Friday. That way, we won't clash. We have to look good, don't we?"

That's right, Alfie thought. The girls should stick together.

"I want to be a mermaid," Phoebe said with a sigh. "Only I can't figure out how to walk around with a mermaid tail. Much less march in a parade," she added, blushing at the idea.

Phoebe blushed more than any other All-Star kid, Alfie reminded herself, watching the color rise in her new friend's cheeks. Even Phoebe's *blushing* made her blush. But kids were getting used to it by now.

"I don't think we actually have to *march*," Alfie said.

"I want to be a superhero," Arletty said. "Like Dragon Girl. Maybe that's what I'll be."

"Dragon Girl is *beautiful*," Phoebe said, glad to have Arletty become the center of attention. Her blush settled down.

Mermaids, Alfie thought. And beautiful superheroes! They sounded so *pretty*.

Bunnies were cute, in Alfie's opinion—but they weren't pretty.

She gave Bella a doubtful look, thinking of the bunny costumes Mrs. Babcock was probably sewing this very minute.

Would they look too babyish?

Maybe wearing a bunny costume wasn't the best way to fit in with the other second-grade girls.

Bella looked perfectly relaxed, happy—and not worried at all. In fact, she was actually munching on a carrot stick from her lunch bag, Alfie saw, dismayed.

Just like a bunny.

Now Alfie could feel her own cheeks get hot.

Bunnies were *very* babyish, she decided, staring down at the picnic table.

"Well, I get to be the princess this year," Suzette announced, fluffing her hair in advance. "The lucky princess. So I'm calling dibs on *that*."

"Nuh-uh," Lulu said, frowning. "You can't call dibs on being the only princess, whether she's lucky or not. Because my mom started making my princess gown last weekend. And I already have a tiara."

Uh-oh, Alfie thought, her heart beating a little faster. Was this going to be another squabble? The second-grade girls had already lived through one or two big ones this year. And it was only October!

"But my mother went out and *bought* my princess costume," Hanni said. "In San Diego," she added, as if that settled the matter. "And it cost a lot of money, too. We can't take it back."

And that's that, she seemed to be saying.

"But I said it first," Suzette said, jumping to her feet, as if ready to fight. "I called dibs."

"So what?" Lulu asked. "I said it second."

"And my princess dress is already hanging in my closet," Hanni said. "You guys don't even have your costumes yet. So be something else."

"No," Suzette said, a stony look on her face. "Being a princess this Halloween is gonna bring me good luck for the whole year, and I'm not switching."

Good luck for the whole year, Alfie thought, impressed. What did that even mean?

Winning every board game you ever played?

Being given extra treat bags at birthday parties?

Discovering buried treasure in your backyard?

Could Suzette be right?

"Well, I don't *care* about your good luck," Lulu said. "Because no way am *I* gonna switch."

The second-grade girls at the picnic table almost vibrated with silence for a moment, watching this standoff. Suzette and Lulu and Hanni were friends, they all knew. But each girl was used to getting her own way.

So what was going to happen next?

"Are you telling me that we're gonna have *three princesses* in our class on Halloween?" Hanni finally asked. "Because that's just silly!"

"It's ridiculous," Lulu said.

"Yeah," Suzette surprised everyone by agreeing. "We can't *all* be princesses, or there won't be anyone left to boss around."

"Well, what are we gonna do?" Hanni asked. "Vote on it?"

"Vote all you want to," Lulu said with a snort. "But I will still be a princess on Halloween. I'm not gonna disappoint my mom."

"Vote your heads off," Suzette chimed in. "But I'm going to be a princess, too. And I'll have good luck for the whole rest of the year."

Good luck with *that*, Alfie thought, grabbing her backpack as the morning buzzer sounded.

Bzzz-z-z!

Taking Sides

"Even the boys know us girls are having an argument," Alfie whispered to Bella the next day, Tuesday. "I mean, it's a *quiet* argument, but it's still an argument," she said.

They were in Mr. Havens's crowded cubby room, getting their lunches out of their backpacks. The small room was so noisy that no one could hear what they were saying.

"Not *all* the girls are arguing about who gets to be princess," Bella pointed out, clutching her lunch bag to her chest so nothing would spill. "We aren't arguing, are we? Just those three girls are."

"But now other girls are taking sides," Alfie said. "Whether they want to or not."

Suzette had snagged poor Arletty to be on her

side—since they had gone to preschool together, Suzette said. And Hanni had glommed on to Phoebe, trying to keep up.

Only Lulu did not yet have an official princess supporter of her own.

"But the boys know there's an argument going on," Bella said. "Even if they don't know what it's about."

"How could they know?" Alfie asked as they made their way into the hall. "We'll never blab. I don't even think Mr. Havens knows what's going on," she added. "Not all the details. But he can tell that *something's* not right," she said as they opened the heavy door and slipped into the noonday light.

And Mr. Havens would speak up before too long, Alfie knew from experience.

The second grade All-Star girls ate lunch at the picnic tables lined up on the raised grassy border surrounding two sides of the main playground behind the school. This playground was where the basketball hoops, tetherball poles, painted kickball squares, swings, and monkey bars were. But after lunch, the girls liked to make their way down a grassy slope to the school's new "nature feature." This was a sunken, shady play area that had two slides—one straight and one curly, as the kindergarten kids put it—and a circle of upright logs.

The girls liked to pretend the logs surrounded an invisible campfire.

It was their favorite hangout.

Up at the picnic tables, though, the sniping had begun. "That's a funny thing for Hanni to eat for lunch," Suzette was telling Arletty—and everyone. "Isn't it, Arletty? Isn't mush inside a little plastic container a funny thing to eat for lunch? It's not something a princess would eat."

"I don't know," Arletty whispered, clearly miserable. Her dark eyes darted from face to face.

Save me! she seemed to be saying.

It looked like Arletty was powerless to resist Suzette.

"Hanni doesn't even throw the mush container away, like a normal person would," Suzette continued with a fake shudder.

"It's yummy hummus," Hanni replied, laughing. "And of *course* I don't throw the container away. I recycle it," she said, as if explaining something to a baby. "That's the cool, princess-y thing to do, Suzette—which is probably why you haven't heard about it yet. Has she, Phoebe?"

"Princesses are too busy to recycle stuff," Suzette informed Hanni.

"No, they aren't," Hanni said. "In fact, they're the ones who usually come up with great ideas like recycling. And everybody copies them after that."

"Oh, I don't know," Lulu said in an airy way from across the table, even though she still hadn't rounded up even one little follower.

Lulu had already been mean once to Bella this semester, Alfie remembered, and so even though she had apologized, Bella was out. And Lulu and Alfie were friends, having even given a party together a few weeks back. But Alfie had no wish to be bossed around today, or any day. By anyone.

And Lulu could be every bit as bossy as Suzette, Alfie knew.

"What don't you know?" Hanni asked, pretending to be polite.

"The point *is*, I don't think you should be saying mean things about a person's lunch," Lulu said. "That's not very princess-y," she explained, using Hanni's earlier word. "Not when you're wearing *that*."

And Lulu pointed at Suzette.

Always-cute Lulu Marino was famous for what she called her "outfits," Alfie thought as she turned to check out what Suzette was wearing that was supposed to be so bad.

Suzette was just wearing regular clothes. And she looked perfectly fine, in Alfie's opinion. Cute, even.

"Wearing what?" Suzette said, inspecting her T-shirt.

"It's just not very fancy, that's all," Lulu said, sounding sorry for Suzette. "And princesses always dress fancy."

"Well, *I'm* dressed okay," Hanni said, speaking up as she faced both her rivals. "Aren't I, Phoebe?"

"*Uh-h-h*," Phoebe moaned, as if something

she'd eaten had just given her tummy trouble.

"Don't ask me stuff!" was what she clearly wanted to say.

Poor Pheeb, Alfie couldn't help but think. Getting trapped this way!

"You should just stay out of this, Hanni," Suzette advised. "It's between me and Lulu now, who gets to be princess."

"Says who?" Hanni asked.

"Says me," Suzette announced, not backing down.

"Princesses don't talk like that," Hanni informed her, wadding up her lunch bag and slam-dunking it into a nearby trash container.

Alfie almost started giggling, but she didn't know why.

"Oh. Like you're such an expert on talking," Suzette scoffed.

"And I'm not staying out of it," Hanni said. "Because my princess gown is already hanging in my closet. Period."

"You already told us," Lulu said. "Nobody cares."

Wow, Alfie thought, throwing away what was

left of her own lunch. That was pretty cold. And Hanni and Lulu used to be friends!

Like, *last week,* Alfie remembered.

And now, every second grade girl's meal had been ruined by all this drama, this quarreling. There wasn't even enough time left to go hang out down at the log circle.

And there were still three days to go before the Halloween celebration.

How long could an argument last?

The Princess Wars

"I have to talk to you," Alfie told EllRay in the family room after dinner that night. "Upstairs. In private," she whispered, although no one was around to hear.

Their dad was in his home office, doing something with rocks, probably. Their mom was looking up recipes at the dining table.

"Yo. It's private *here*," EllRay pointed out. He was sprawled on the sectional, Princess in his lap and a copy of *Sports Illustrated* in his hands. He had just finished his "Ratios and Fractions" worksheet. It lay on the table in front of him. Alfie flopped down in an easy chair.

EllRay had been trying to flick through some magazine pages without disturbing the sleeping kitten, but he paused to look at his sister. "What's up, Alf? You in trouble again?" he teased, his brows rising—just like their dad's eyebrows did when *he* asked a question.

"Let's go upstairs," Alfie said again. "Mom might come in."

"She won't," EllRay told her. "She's trying to figure out what snack to make for our class parties on Friday. You know she hates to cook," he added. "But she says it's supposed to be something homemade and healthy. So, are you in trouble?" he asked once more, frowning.

"Nuh-uh," Alfie told him, shaking her head. "But some girls in my class are fighting—in secret. Three of them. And I just wanted to talk to you about it, not Mom," she added, glancing toward the door. "Or it will turn into this big *thing*."

Sometimes, talking to EllRay was the best solution, in Alfie's opinion. Her big brother could be a pain, but she and EllRay were basically a team. Except you couldn't be boring or whiny around him, Alfie reminded herself.

And he hated it if you cried.

"Okay," EllRay said, setting aside the magazine. "Talk."

Alfie took a deep breath. "Well, those three girls I was telling you about all want to be the same thing for Halloween. A princess."

"Shocker," EllRay said, not even trying to hide his grin. "So, let them. What do you care?"

"I don't care at all," Alfie said. "But now they're making other girls in our class take sides. I'm afraid they're gonna ruin the big day," she tried to explain. "I mean, by Friday, nobody will be talking to anyone else. None of the girls, I mean."

And those were the main kids she cared about.

"Are *you* taking sides?" EllRay asked.

"No," Alfie said, staring at EllRay's worksheet. But there was still tomorrow and the next day to get through, Wednesday and Thursday. And Lulu had been circling her like a shark all afternoon, determined trap at least one All-Star girl to be on her side.

"And what are *you* gonna be on Friday?" Ell-Ray asked.

"That's not the point," Alfie told him, not wanting to say "a bunny," or explain about her new friend Bella. Because by now, with the secret princess wars going on, bunnies really did sound kind of babyish.

Anyway, EllRay would find out soon enough, she thought, scowling—at Oak Glen Primary School's Halloween parade on Friday.

He would probably feel embarrassed for her, or, worse, tease her.

"Then what *is* the point?" EllRay asked.

"How do I stay out of the princess wars until Friday—and still keep all my friends?" Alfie asked. "I mean, do all the girls in *your* class still get dragged into fights? Do they even fight anymore?"

"Are you kidding me?" EllRay said, laughing. "They stealth-fight all the time! Not *loud*, and not all of them. But their feuds can last for ages."

"Like, tell me about one of them," Alfie said, leaning toward him.

"Hmm," EllRay said, thinking. "Well, these two girls Teresa and Natty are still mad at each other about something that happened *last year*, in fifth grade. They're always trying to get even with each other."

"But do Nessa and Tatty make the other girls in your class take sides?" Alflie asked, trying to work the conversation back to *her* problem.

"Teresa and Natty," EllRay corrected her. "And they would if they could, I'm sure," he added.

Alfie nodded.

"But a couple of weeks ago, " EllRay continued, "our teacher gave the whole class this talk about how lame it was to treat your hurt feelings like they were your most valuable stuff. Something like that. And we all knew who he was talking about. So that made those girls stop for a while, mostly because Teresa and Natty know the rest of us don't want to get yelled at again."

"He yelled at you guys?" Alfie said, her eyes big as she attempted to picture the scene. Sixth grade sounded so harsh!

"Not exactly," EllRay said. "But you get the idea."

Alfie nodded. She tried to imagine Mr. Havens doing something like that.

It was pretty easy, actually.

"So, how do I stay out of the princess wars?" Alfie asked again, thinking of Lulu, and those hungry shark eyes staring at her from behind her perfectly straight bangs.

"Just do something else when those three girls start arguing," EllRay suggested. "You could do that easy for two days, I bet. You could do it standing on your head."

"What?" Alfie asked, alarmed.

"Chill," EllRay said, laughing. "It's just an expression, Alfie. *Ouch*," he added as Princess woke, stretched, and started sharpening her little claws on his leg.

"She probably thinks you're a tree, you're so tall," Alfie said, watching them. "Can Princess sleep with me tonight?"

"I don't know," EllRay said, carrying the kitten over to the scratching post in the corner of the room. "You're gonna have to work that out with *her*."

"Okay, fine," Alfie said, copying Princess's stretch. "And thanks for helping me," she added, remembering to be polite.

Her big brother hadn't really helped *much*, in her opinion.

But there would always be a next time, she knew—because that was one thing about problems.

You could always count on them to keep turning up.

10

Alfie's Idea

Uh-oh, Alfie thought on Wednesday morning, shortly after Mr. Havens finished taking attendance. He was perched on the edge of his desk, one long leg swinging as he thought. He straightened his narrow tie.

An uneasy silence filled the room. What was up?

Alfie counted to ten as she stared at her teacher's big foot, afraid to look him in the eye. Did Mr. Havens have to shop for shoes at a special store? she wondered. Not a store that sold clown shoes. His feet weren't *that* big. But they were bigger than most feet, that was for sure.

Maybe you had to have gigantic feet in order to play basketball, Alfie thought.

Why wasn't he saying anything?

"It has come to my attention that you All-Stars have a problem brewing," Mr. Havens finally said.

Alfie held her breath and tried to look innocent. Well, she *was* innocent, she reminded herself! *She* hadn't done anything wrong. It was the princess girls who were messing things up— Suzette, Hanni, and Lulu.

Maybe Mr. Havens wasn't even talking about the girls, Alfie thought in a flash, watching the boys in her class start to squirm as they listened to their teacher's words. Seated next to her, Scooter was trying to catch Bryan's eye across the room. And opposite her, poor Alan looked like he was about to faint.

What had those bad boys done?

Alfie tried to remember different pranks Ell-Ray had told her about.

Had the boys taped shut the light switches?

Had they stretched plastic wrap over the toilet seats in the boys' room?

Had they swiped Mr. Havens's dreaded red marking pen?

"This only involves the All-Star girls, though," Mr. Havens said, and half the class sighed with relief. "So I think I'll save my little talk for them—during morning recess," he went on. "You girls will stay inside with me, please."

"*Aww*," came the disappointed girls' chorus, led by Arletty, who was the fastest runner in class—girl *or* boy. Recesses and lunchtime were never complete for her until she had run a couple of laps around either the big playground, or the school's new lower playground.

"Woo-hoo!" Scooter said, trying to high-five a reluctant Alan.

"That's enough of that, Mr. Davis," Mr. Havens told Scooter. "Unless you'd like to stay inside with the girls after Writing Workshop, that is."

"No thanks, Coach," Scooter said, sitting up straight in his chair.

And his teacher just sighed and shook his head.

* * *

"Bottoms in chairs," Mr. Havens barked at the girls at recess, after they had gotten their morning snacks from the cubby room. Just for today, they'd be allowed to eat in class, he had told them. But *no crumbs*.

The girls took their seats. Mr. Havens loosened his tie, as if doing so might help him figure out where to begin.

"This better be good," Lulu muttered—but not softly enough.

"We'll start with you, Miss Marino," Mr. Havens said, turning to face Lulu. "A little bird has told me that you, Hanni, and Suzette have been squabbling over who gets to be a princess at the parade and party on Friday. The day after tomorrow," he reminded everyone.

Just two more days!

Alfie couldn't believe someone had blabbed—about something as silly as this. Halloween costumes?

Probably a worried parent, she guessed. A *new* parent, maybe.

"Is squabbling the same thing as fighting?" Bella asked after raising her hand.

"It is," Mr. Havens said, nodding. "And I'm not having it. Do you girls hear me?" he asked.

This was not the kind of question that needed an answer, in Alfie's opinion.

But Lulu's chin came up, a sure sign with her that she was not about to give in. "Well, my mom is almost done making my gown," she told Mr. Havens. "A gown is a princess dress, by the way," she informed him. "But that's why I should get to be the princess this year."

"But me and my mom already bought my costume," Hanni objected, her face turning pink with anger. "In San Diego. For a lot of money! So *for sure* I can't be anything else for Halloween, and Phoebe agrees with me. My mom would have a conniption fit."

She would, too, Alfie thought, picturing Mrs. Sobel getting the bad news.

"It's 'my mom and I,' not 'me and my mom,'" Mr. Havens told Hanni—but Hanni just stared at him.

"But I called dibs first on being a princess," Suzette argued. "Arletty even heard me do it. Didn't you, Arletty?"

Looking horrified, Arletty gave the world's tiniest nod.

"And a princess costume is the perfect thing for me this year, Mr. Havens," Suzette continued. "It'll bring me luck all year long if I wear it. And I really need good luck."

Suzette had said this twice! Alfie wondered why.

"Would you say it's bringing you good luck now?" Mr. Havens asked, tilting his muscle-y head.

"Well, not *now*," Suzette admitted. "But today's not Halloween."

"Neither is Friday," Mr. Havens said. "So wear your princess dress on the thirty-first. On Tuesday. And wear it Friday, too, if you want," he added, shrugging. "All of you. I'm sure each one of you girls already has a tiara."

All the girls in class nodded. Alfie had two! Tiaras—unlike some barrettes—looked wonderful on every girl. On every kind of hair.

"But—but—but—" Suzette spluttered.

"Three princesses?" Lulu wailed.

"That's impossible!" Hanni cried.

"But wait," Alfie said, her voice sounding way too loud.

"Wait for what?" Hanni snapped.

"Hold on, Miss Sobel," Mr. Havens said. "Let Alfie speak."

"It's just that there are a ton of princesses in the world," Alfie said, feeling her face grow hot as everyone stared at her. "From all over the place. Lots more than three, that's for sure. I saw a show about it on TV. So why couldn't our class have lots of princesses, too?"

Everyone was staring at her.

"There's no law that says we couldn't *all* be princesses," Alfie continued, her heart pounding as she made her point. "If we wanted to, I mean."

Princess Alfie, she thought suddenly, a picture popping into her head.

"That's just silly, Alfie," Suzette said with a sniff.

"Yeah," Hanni agreed. "It's impossible," she said—for the second time.

"Of course it's not impossible," Mr. Havens said, getting to his feet. "As far as I'm concerned, Alfie just had a great idea. You *are* all princesses, ladies. Each and every All-Star girl sitting here in front of me. The sweet princesses, the funny princesses, the quiet princesses, even the crabby ones. So I'm with Alfie on this one. If you all want to dress up like princesses on Friday, go for it."

"Wait a minute," Hanni said, actually holding up her hand like a cartoon policeman. "All *thirteen* of us?"

"Each and every one of you," Mr. Havens repeated. "Just like Alfie said. Why not?"

Why not? Alfie echoed silently.

Bella and her mom, that was why not.

"But—that's impossible," Suzette said, stealing Hanni's earlier line.

"Of course it's not impossible," Mr. Havens said. "You can form a princess team, as far as I'm concerned. A princess posse. You can all link arms and do a princess dance."

That sounded like fun!

By now, Hanni, Lulu, and Suzette looked as if they thought that maybe three princesses might have been okay, after all. But thirteen?

Unconcerned, Bella doodled in her notebook. She glanced at Alfie, holding up two fingers—*like bunny ears*.

Trying to ignore her, Alfie's mind raced as she imagined the perfect princess gown. Something shiny, she thought—and long, with sparkles.

"What if I want to be something else, though, Mr. Havens?" Arletty asked. "Like Dragon Girl?"

"Or a mermaid?" Phoebe said, almost squeaking out the words.

"You don't *have* to be a princess," Mr. Havens assured her—and everyone. "Does she, Alfie? Any girl here can be anything she wants on Friday," he said, obviously eager to wrap things up. "Within the school dress code and the bounds of good taste, of course," he added. "You girls will change into your costumes after lunch in the girls' room. And away you'll go."

The only part of the dress code that Alfie could remember was "No flip-flops." But princesses, Dragon Girls, mermaids, and bunnies didn't wear flip-flops, so that should be okay.

"And no more squabbling, either," Mr. Havens warned. "Or we can call the whole thing off for *all* you girls. The parade, the party, the works."

The girls gasped. Could he do that?

Probably, knowing him, Alfie thought.

"So, I'd like you to tidy your desks now," Mr. Havens was saying. "And clean up *every last crumb,* as I said before. I do *not* want to receive a note from the custodian. After that, you girls should still have time to go to the restroom and wash up before we get going with our 'Odd and Even Numbers' lesson plan."

The girls got stiffly to their feet, as if they hadn't walked in a very long time.

"Thanks a lot, *Alfie,*" Suzette muttered on the way out the door.

"Yeah, Alfie," Lulu chimed in. "Thanks a lot."

"You're welcome a lot," Alfie said, her heart pounding.

It had been a very good idea, she thought, trying to convince herself.

A *very* good idea.

11

Please?

"You're chatty tonight," Alfie's mom said after dinner. She had just started the dishwasher, and Alfie was sitting in a swivel chair at the kitchen island, swiping every so often at the shiny island surface with a dish towel.

EllRay was in his room, and Dr. Jakes was at a meeting at his college in San Diego.

"I like to talk, I guess," Alfie said. But really, she was trying to figure out how to ask her mother to make her a princess costume—in time for the parade and party on Friday.

That had been a good idea she'd had in class, no matter what Lulu and Suzette thought.

The right words about the costume hadn't

come out yet, though, or anything close to the right words. Alfie knew how busy her mom was lately.

"Did you finish all your homework?" Mrs. Jakes asked.

"Mm-hmm," Alfie said, nodding.

And swiveling.

And swiping.

Her mom called that "multitasking."

"It was mostly a Science Activities worksheet tonight," Alfie explained, thinking she should say more. "It was called 'Classifying Our Animal Pals.' You know, like whether the animals are mammals, reptiles, birds, or amphibians," she added, struggling a little over the last word.

She kept saying "amphubians" by mistake, or "amphlibians."

"Did you even *know* all those guys were animals, Mom?" Alfie added. "Because when I was little, I thought animals had to have fur."

"Mmm," her mother said, half listening. "Did you look up all the words?"

"We didn't have to *define* them," Alfie said.

"We just had to draw lines from the words to the little drawings of the animals. And I think I got everything right."

"That's excellent," her mother said, glancing at the microwave clock.

Yeesh, Alfie thought. Her mom was about to go take a look at her writing! And this was important.

Do something fast, she told herself. "Listen, Mom," she began.

The kitchen was silent for a moment.

"Yes?" Mrs. Jakes finally asked. "Just spit it out, sweetie," she said, meaning that Alfie should say what was on her mind, Alfie knew. Not that she should actually spit anything out.

Gak.

And so Alfie decided to go for it. She hopped down from the swivel chair and adjusted her T-shirt. "Listen, Mom," she said again. "I really want to be a princess on Friday." She tried to make this statement sound reasonable and urgent at the same time. "I *need* to be a princess. So can you make me a princess dress in time? Please? I mean a gown," Alfie corrected herself. "Because that's what they call a dress when a princess is wearing it."

"Alfieta Jakes," her mother said, shocked. "You told me you were all set for Friday. I just assumed you were going with that darling bumblebee costume."

Oops, Alfie thought, thinking instantly of an entirely different costume: the bunny costume Mrs. Babcock was sewing for her.

This very minute, maybe!

Whir-r-r-r! Alfie could almost hear the sound of a sewing machine.

She had forgotten all about it—for the second time today.

The first time she forgot, Alfie had tried out the princess idea on Bella during lunch. "My princess idea sounds like fun, doesn't it?" she had asked. "Dressing up all poofy and everything. With sparkles and a tiara," she added, her own eyes shining.

They could blend in with everyone else.

Her wish come true!

"Yeah, but we're all set," Bella reminded her through a bite of sandwich.

Oh, yeah, Alfie thought, her princess dream sinking into a puddle of gloom.

But the dream had returned.

Alfie had not said *one word* to her mom or dad about the bunny costume in the four days that had passed since her playdate with Bella. The only time she even thought of saying anything about it to them was last night at bedtime, but she decided it would be more fun to keep the bunny costume secret.

That wasn't lying, she assured herself—it was planning a surprise.

And she sure wasn't going to say anything now that she had changed her mind! Because—*she wanted to be a princess*, Alfie told herself firmly. Like Suzette, Hanni, and Lulu. And probably also like Phoebe, and at least two of the other girls, too, Nina and Estella, which meant "star."

The whole princess thing had been her bright idea! She *deserved* to be a princess. So Bella could be "all set" about being a bunny all by herself.

Bella was tough, Alfie told herself. She could take it.

Ping! She felt the tiniest tickle of guilt.

"Alfie?" her mother was saying—as if for the fourth or fifth time. "What happened to you being a darling little bumblebee?"

"I just can't, Mom," Alfie said, sudden tears filling her eyes.

"But—but this is Wednesday night, sweetie," her mom said. "And your party is on Friday. That would only give me one day, *tomorrow*, to make you

a princess gown. And I'm already supposedly making two batches of homemade pumpkin muffins. *And* I'm in the middle of a writing project—with a deadline."

"I know, Mom," Alfie said, sniffling as she wrapped her arms around her mother, trying to dab her eyes dry on Mrs. Jakes's already-damp apron.

"Don't you dare wipe your nose on my apron, Miss Alfie," her mother cautioned, laughing. "We have tissues for that sort of thing."

"I know," Alfie said again. "And I'm sorry

about the costume, Mom. I didn't know we were all going to be princesses, did I? So, *please*?" she asked again.

"Since when do you care what everyone else is doing, young lady?" her mother asked, holding Alfie at arm's length for a moment so she could take a good look at her. "You're one of a kind, you are."

That was probably what all moms thought about their kids, Alfie thought. But really, "one of a kind" was not what she wanted to be.

"I know, Mom," she said. "But this is different. It's like everyone was arguing, see," she tried to explain. "Only now, we're all on the same side, thanks to me."

Or they would be, once things settled down, Alfie told herself.

But how could she explain to her mom how important the princess costume was, Alfie thought, when she couldn't even explain it to herself?

"Hmm," her mother began. "Well, that proves I was right about your leadership skills, I suppose. And I *guess* I can remember wanting something so badly that I couldn't really think of anything else."

"Like me," Alfie said. "Wanting something sparkly," she added, hinting.

"And I *guess* I could put a princess gown together tomorrow," Mrs. Jakes said. "Those pumpkin muffins might not get baked here at home, but I can always pick up something at the supermarket."

"Yummy," Alfie said, encouraging her.

"Says you," her mother said with a laugh.

Well, yeah, Alfie thought. She was the only person in the kitchen, wasn't she? Who else was gonna say something?

"Okay. You're on," Alfie's mother said, giving her daughter a squeeze. "I'm not promising any miracles, Alfie. But I'll try to do a good job on that gown."

"Thanks, Mom," Alfie said, hugging her again. "You're the best."

"You're telling me," her mother said with a laugh. "Sometimes I amaze even myself!"

12

Secret

"It's your day to carpool, Mom," Alfie announced at breakfast the next day, Thursday.

"Why do you look so worried?" her mother asked as she wrapped a second breakfast burrito for EllRay. "I've never missed carpool yet, have I? And after I drop you and Hanni off at school, I'm heading out to buy the fabric for your costume."

"Some *fancy* fabric," Alfie said, sneaking a peek at her brother to see if he was impressed.

Nope. He just continued to chew.

"Some fancy fabric for a *princess* gown," Alfie said. But EllRay was too busy taking another giant bite out of his burrito even to listen, it seemed. "But, Mom," Alfie added, lowering her voice. "Please don't mention anything about the gown to Hanni, okay? Because—*it's a secret*," she said, whispering the last words.

This wasn't the real reason she didn't want Hanni to find out about her costume plans, Alfie admitted to herself—even though every All-Star girl was now officially allowed to be a princess, thanks to her. But Hanni might still be blaming her for that, Alfie knew. And Thursdays seemed like very long days already. Having Hanni stomping around and glaring at her would make this one even longer.

Tomorrow, Friday, would be soon enough for Hanni to find out.

EllRay's head popped up. "Why don't you want Hanni to know you're gonna be a princess tomorrow?" he asked. "Why is it a secret?"

This had to be the part of the conversation he heard?

Alfie scowled. "I wasn't talking to you," she told her brother.

"Alfie," her mother warned.

"Okay, sorry," Alfie said. *"But I wasn't,"* she whispered to EllRay as their mom washed her hands at the kitchen sink.

"Who even cares?" EllRay shot back as he grabbed his backpack and headed out the kitchen door.

✳ ✳ ✳

It was a cool morning, and Alfie was secretly glad her mom had made her wear a sweater to school. She hadn't even argued, for once, because of the whole princess-gown thing.

"My hair's getting messed up from the wind," Hanni complained, stepping out of the Jakes's car. She narrowed her green eyes and scowled at the sky as she spoke. "And now we're gonna have to say hi to Principal James," she added, as if this were the final straw.

Alfie was barely listening to Hanni, though. She was too busy scanning the school steps for Bella. She had to say something to her newest friend about the princess costume, but what should she say?

So far, she hadn't actually lied to *anyone*, Alfie assured herself.

And she hadn't hurt anybody's feelings.

But it was like she was floating inside a bubble

that was about to pop, Alfie knew. Because tomorrow, her costume secret would be revealed to everyone, especially Bella. And to her mom. And to Bella's mom.

Princess Alfie, she thought again, trying to picture it.

Maybe she should try again to get Bella to be a princess, too!

But right this very minute, Alfie thought, Bella was probably imagining how great it was going to be tomorrow, with the two of them surprising everyone with their funny bunny costumes.

How could friends have such different dreams?

And in another part of Oak Glen, Alfie's already-too-busy mom might be parking her car outside the fabric store while her lonely laptop—with its story inside—waited at home.

And at Bella's house, cheerful Mrs. Babcock was probably stitching the silky insides of bunny ears onto fleece, if a person could even do that.

And all Alfie could do was to daydream about being a princess.

Was that such a bad thing?

"No!" Alfie said aloud in the crowded hall. But

Hanni didn't hear her. She had already charged ahead like a bouncy-haired bulldozer-girl.

Sure, *Hanni* was happy, Alfie told herself, frowning. Hanni got to be a princess who didn't feel guilty.

Alfie pushed her way through the door to the playground and stepped into the windy morning once more.

This is all Bella's fault, she thought, starting to get mad.

Sure-of-herself Bella, whose bright idea it had been to be a bunny in the first place—in a class full of beautiful Dragon Girls, mermaids, and maybe even a *quinceañera* pretend-teenager or two wearing dresses that looked like they were made out of puffy pink clouds.

Bella, who she, Alfie, had invited to be a beautiful princess just yesterday. "With sparkles and a tiara," she had said.

But oh, no! Not Bella, who liked to go her own way.

"Thanks a lot, *Bella*," Alfie whispered.

Almost Heart-to-Heart

"*Hup, hup*, listen up," Mr. Havens told his class after he had put away the All-Stars' current Shared Reading book. Alfie had barely heard a word of the book, she was so worried about morning recess—and facing Bella.

What was she going to say to her?

"It's Writing Workshop time," Mr. Havens reminded everyone. "We will continue our unit on Opinion Writing. So, pencils and paper out, please. *Quietly.*"

The kids at each table rummaged through their plastic containers of supplies while Mr. Havens printed some words on the board. "Not *this* again," one boy grumbled softly.

"Yes, this again, Bryan," Mr. Havens said,

turning around. "And our topic for today is 'What Is Your Opinion?' But first, let's review. I want each of you to write down one fact about your bedroom. A fact, not an opinion."

Alfie thought, then wrote, *There is one desk in my bedroom.*

"What did you write?" Scooter whispered, a lock of hair flopping over his forehead. "I can't think of anything."

"Just put down something real," Alfie whispered back. "Like, write down how many windows your room has," she suggested.

"*Shhh,*" Hanni scolded from the other side of the table. No cheating!"

"I never counted my windows," Scooter said, scowling. "Why would I?"

"And now," Mr. Havens said, giving Alfie's table a look, "I want you to write down one *opinion* about your bedroom. And remember, an opinion is a belief or a feeling. It's your personal point of view. And if you look at the board, I have written some ways to begin 'opinion sentences' for this topic," he continued. "Just as a reminder."

Alfie stared at the board.

"I think..."

"I feel..."

"Every bedroom should..."

"In my opinion..."

Were they supposed to use *all* of them? She'd better get busy!

In my opinion, Alfie wrote, printing as fast as she could, *I feel that my bedroom should have a fuzzy zebra-skin rug. I* <u>*think.*</u>

Phew!

"Bryan?" Mr. Havens said. "Since you're so talkative today, let's hear your opinion about your bedroom."

"Me?" Bryan almost squawked, looking astonished. "I didn't finish yet, but here goes. '*My bedroom should have a big TV and bunk beds with a slide and a popcorn maker. In my opinion.*'"

"That sounds pretty complete to me," Mr. Havens said with a smile. "Now, who wants to go next?"

And on they went—until the buzzer for morning recess set them free.

* * *

"I wanted to talk to you this morning before school," Bella said to Alfie in the cubby room as they reached into their backpacks for their morning snacks. "Only I couldn't find you. You didn't come to the picnic tables. Were you late for school?"

"No," Alfie said, shaking her head. "I decided to go down to the log circle, for a change. Sorry."

"You went down there all alone?" Bella asked, puzzled.

"Yeah," Alfie said, trying for a casual shrug. She did not want to admit the truth—that she'd been hiding out. "Sometimes I do that," she told Bella. "I like to watch the kindergarten kids play on the slides. Why?" she asked. "What did you want to talk about?"

"I have some really good news," Bella said, her golden eyes sparkling. "My mom finished both our bunny costumes late last night, and she said I could ask you over after school, so you can try yours on. We can call your mother from the office," she said, still smiling.

Oh, no, Alfie thought. She was not even going to *wear* the bunny costume tomorrow. But she didn't want to lie to Bella and pretend she *was* going to wear it.

The best thing was to keep stalling, Alfie told herself—because so far, no lies. And lying is wrong, she reminded herself silently.

Stalling was not going to work forever, Alfie knew, but she didn't know what else to do. She was "in a pickle," as her mother would say.

But she *was* going to be a princess tomorrow!

"I can't come over today," Alfie told Bella, trying to invent a good excuse—fast. "Because tonight's a school night, see. And—"

"I know it's a school night," Bella interrupted. "But some of the kids in our class were saying we won't have any homework tonight. You know, because of the parade and party tomorrow. Come on, Alfie," she added, a funny look on her face.

Uh-oh.

"Will you be mad at me if I don't come over?" Alfie asked as the last lingering kid left the cubby room. "Because you always seem so okay about everything. Nothing much ever bothers you, Bella, and that's so cool. Not like with Phoebe and the ladybugs," she added, searching for an example. "Or like Alan being called on in class. I wish nothing ever bothered *me*," she added, looking away.

It was true. Sometimes *everything* bothered her, Alfie thought.

Being asked to take out the trash when it wasn't her turn.

Having on the wrong color top when all her friends were wearing pink.

Hearing one of the All-Star girls say that she had a secret.

Bella looked surprised. "Some stuff bothers me," she said quietly. "Like when my mom told me all of a sudden that we had to move to Oak Glen. I had already started second grade in Ventura, see. I've moved three times since preschool!" she added, her forehead wrinkling.

Three times? Wow!

Alfie could still picture the unpacked boxes in the Babcocks' spare room. Bella had entered Oak Glen Primary School one month after the semester started, she remembered. That must have been hard.

She and Bella were having what her mom

called a "heart-to-heart talk," Alfie realized, surprised. Or *almost* heart-to-heart. Because it wasn't as if she were telling Bella everything.

"But moving is a *big* thing," she said to Bella, trying to push these thoughts aside. "I mean, moving that fast would bother any kid in the world. I'm talking about how *small stuff* never bothers you. Like, if one of the boys squirts your water at the drinking fountain during recess. Or if Suzette starts whispering to Lulu right in front of you, and then she tells you to mind your own business if you even look at them."

Or if a new friend decides on a costume change at the last minute, Alfie added to herself. She crossed her fingers and hoped this last example was also true.

"*Hmm*," Bella said. "Well, as long as you make friends with someone after you move, you're okay. But until that happens," she added, "you just have to learn how to hang out by yourself—because making friends can be hard when you start school late. Kids already have friends by then, see. They've probably known each other since forever. That's why I'm so glad about you and me, Alfie," she added, suddenly shy.

Ouch.

But she *was* going to be a princess tomorrow, Alfie repeated silently.

"How come you guys have to move so much?" she asked Bella, mostly to change the subject. She and her friends didn't usually ask questions about each other's parents and their decisions. But Bella had brought it up.

"Because of my dad's job," Bella said, shrugging as her suddenly nervous fingers tidied a few things in someone's cubby. Not her own. As her face had paled, the freckles on Bella's nose were more visible than before, Alfie noticed.

"*Scooter Davis*," she whispered, reading aloud the masking tape name on the cubby.

She'd never tell on Bella, though, Alfie told herself—and Scooter was usually so worn out after recess that he probably wouldn't notice.

He didn't even know how many windows there were in his own bedroom!

"But I guess you're right, Alfie," Bella said with another shrug. "Maybe the small stuff *doesn't* bother me as much as it does other kids. I mean, maybe I can't let it, can I?"

"How come you can't?" Alfie asked. "Because you're so worried about bigger stuff happening? Like having to move again?"

"Something like that," Bella said, but then she brightened. "We're gonna have so much fun tomorrow!"

"Yeah," Alfie said. "No matter *what* we wear, right? But listen, Bella," she continued. "I told my mom I'd help her with something at home after school." Her heart pounded as she fibbed. "And plus, she's driving carpool today," Alfie added. "She has to come to school and get Hanni anyway. So I'd better go home with them."

There, Alfie thought, her face burning. Those were two *very good reasons* why she couldn't try on the bunny costume Mrs. Babcock had made for her.

Not that either of the reasons solved her basic problem, which was telling Bella she was not even going to *be* a bunny.

But at least that terrible moment was postponed for a while.

Alfie did not like the confused look on Bella's face. "Look, Bella," she continued, tugging at her friend's sweater to distract her. "There's still a few minutes of recess left. Let's go outside and play."

"Okay. I *guess*," Bella said slowly. She was tilting her head as she looked at Alfie. "Is everything okay?" she asked.

"Everything is absolutely perfect," Alfie said, trying not to burst into tears.

Why did Bella have to be so *nice*?

"Look, Bella," Alfie said again. "I'm sorry about after school. But I'm sure the bunny costume will fit just fine when I wear it tomorrow." She crossed her fingers behind her back.

Okay, she told herself—now she was coming pretty close to lying.

She was right next door to it, in fact.

"I guess the costume will fit," Bella said slowly. "I mean, you're little, and the costume is big. But it's really cute," she added, in case Alfie was having any doubts. "And listen, Alfie. I'm just so happy we're gonna be bunnies together for my first Oak Glen Halloween."

"Yeah," Alfie said, and she tried not to think anymore about disappointing her new friend with this one *very small thing*.

Bella could "hang out by herself" a while longer, couldn't she?

Because she, Alfie Jakes, had her own dreams! Her own life to live. And that life involved princess gowns—and having good luck for the rest of the year.

"So like I was saying," Alfie continued, "let's go outside and play. Okay?" she asked again, giving Bella's sweater another tug.

Alfie and EllRay

"Hey, EllRay," Alfie said that night after dinner as she poked her head into her brother's room. "Did you ever lie to a friend? Or *almost* lie," she quickly corrected herself.

"Why would I?" EllRay said from where he and Princess lay sprawled on the bed.

"I dunno," Alfie said. "So you wouldn't hurt their feelings?"

"But lying to someone would be worse than hurting their feelings," EllRay pointed out. "Because you'd be tricking them. And they'd probably find out about it. Anyway, how do you 'almost lie'?" he asked, giving Alfie a suspicious look.

"You might leave out part of the truth by mistake," Alfie said, thinking fast. "Or you could pretend you're gonna do something, only you're really not. You don't *promise* to do it, though. Not, like, cross-your-heart. So that's not really a lie," she announced.

"I think it kind of is," EllRay said, laughing. "I mean, how would you feel if someone treated you that way?"

Whoa, Alfie thought, catching her breath. She would definitely feel bad if a friend even *half* lied to her.

"I would feel not good," she admitted. "Unless my friend was lying to make me feel better about something," she added, hope glimmering.

"Huh," EllRay said. "It would still be a lie."

"What about if your friend gets a bad haircut," Alfie asked, desperate for a way out, "and they ask if they look okay? What about then?"

"You tell them, 'Hair grows,'" EllRay said. "I said that to Marco once."

Alfie sighed. This must be one of those things where it was different for boys, she thought, flopping down onto the shaggy rug next to Ell-Ray's desk.

"Make yourself comfortable, why don't you?" EllRay pretended to complain.

But really, Alfie and EllRay were friends. She could count on him, and he could count on her.

"Well, what about luck?" Alfie asked her brother. "Do you believe in luck?"

"Not anymore," EllRay said, laughing. He tossed the graphic novel he'd been reading into the air as if his own luck had just run out, thanks to his little sister showing up.

"No. I mean it," Alfie said.

"I believe in *bad* luck, I guess," EllRay said, stretching his long arms over his head. "Like when you lose a game that you should have won," he explained. "Or when you mess up a whole *bunch* of games, like when you're on a losing streak."

"Huh," Alfie said, thinking.

"Coach says it all evens out in the end," EllRay said, shrugging. "Only sometimes, I'm not so sure."

EllRay's "Coach" was Alfie's "Mr. Havens," of course.

"What about good luck? Do you believe in that?" Alfie asked, combing the rug's strands of yarn with her fingers.

EllRay thought for a few seconds. "Marco believes in good luck," he said, smiling. "Because he has this pair of lucky socks, according to him. And sometimes he wears them on game day, even if they're dirty."

"Yuck," Alfie said. "He's the one without any sisters, right?" she asked. "Because a sister would definitely tell him when he stinks."

"He might not care," EllRay said. "If it was a big enough game."

"But I'm talking about *real* good luck," Alfie said, getting back to her original question. "Do you believe in that?"

"What would you call good luck?" EllRay asked. "Winning a goldfish in a ping-pong ball toss at the San Diego County Fair? Or not breaking your arm when you're trying to do some awesome stunt, only you go flying off your bike? Or messing up during recess, but your parents don't find out? Or buying a raffle ticket at Oak Glen Primary School's Harvest Festival and winning a pie?"

"What kind of pie?" Alfie asked, interested. "Because apple pie would be good luck, but rhubarb pie would be bad luck." She made a face, remembering the surprise sourness of a bite she'd once been offered.

No fair tricking kids that way!

"Some people like rhubarb pie," EllRay argued, scratching Princess under her furry gray chin. The kitten's purring seemed to fill the room.

"No, they don't," Alfie said. "They're just pretending. Lying," she added, saying the dreaded word aloud once more.

EllRay sighed. "If you say so," he said. "But how come you're asking me this stuff?"

"Because, remember Suzette Monahan?" Alfie asked, deciding to explain her problem—but only a little. Not the part about the costume mess—or the almost-lie she was almost telling Bella Babcock.

There was no way she could make that sound good, Alfie was beginning to see.

"How could I forget Suzette?" EllRay said, laughing again. Suzette Monahan had been famous in the Jakes family since Alfie's preschool days. She was the kid who demanded a trip to a fast food restaurant during the girls' first playdate.

Alfie's mom was still smiling and shaking her head over that one.

"Suzette said she heard that if you wear the right costume for Halloween, you get to have good luck for the whole year," Alfie informed her brother. "She said that to Mr. Havens and everyone," she added, as if this somehow made Suzette's claim more believable.

Now EllRay was the one shaking his head. "Where does Suzette come up with this goofy stuff?" he asked Princess.

Purr. Purrr. Purrr-r-r-r.

"So you don't think it's true about luck?" she asked her brother, inspecting a freshly combed patch of rug. She tried to sound as if she didn't care too much one way or the other.

"Of course it's not true," EllRay said. "Suzette was just showing off, or something. Why? You don't believe her, do you?" he asked, frowning.

"I guess not," Alfie said, still not looking at her brother. "It *could* be true, though. I mean, maybe it is, and maybe it isn't."

"Yo, look, Alf," EllRay told his sister. "Why does Suzette have to go and mess up a fun day by making up goofy stuff about good luck for the whole year? That's just wrong. She ruins everything."

"Don't get mad at *me*," Alfie said, raising her voice. "I'm not the one who said it! And you just told me that Marco believes in magic dirty socks," she said even louder. "He's your best friend, in case you forgot. So are you saying Marco's a liar, too?"

"Marco believes in lucky *socks*," EllRay argued. "Period. It's not the same thing as magic at all. *Or* lying."

But Alfie was still angry. "You just told me that when you mess up at school, like at recess, and your parents don't find out, that's good luck," she told her brother. "You said! And it's kind of like lying not to tell them the truth. So are you a liar, too?"

"Me?" EllRay asked, confused.

"You heard me," Alfie said.

It felt good to spread the guilt around a little!

"Why? What did you do wrong at school?" EllRay asked, pouncing on Alfie's words. "How did you mess up?"

"*Stop talking*," Alfie yelled.

"What is going on in here?" their father's voice boomed. He stepped into EllRay's room—sending Princess diving for cover under the bed. "You two are supposed to be quieting down before bedtime, not picking a fight with each other."

"Sorry, Dad," EllRay said.

"Sorry," Alfie mumbled.

"So?" Dr. Jakes said. "What *is* going on in here?" he asked again. "What's the problem?"

Alfie and EllRay swapped super-fast looks. It was as if her brother—her *team*—was asking her how much he should say, Alfie thought.

"Nothing's going on, Dad," she said. "I was just asking EllRay a question about school, that's all."

"Only she didn't like my answer," EllRay said as if he were finishing Alfie's sentence for her.

"Well, I've been *there* before," Dr. Jakes said. But he was still eyeing the two of them with some suspicion. "Tell you what," he said, clearly deciding something on the spot. "EllRay, you stay here in your room with our invisible cat. Miss Alfie will come down to the family room with me to say goodnight to Mom. You can tell *us* what's on your mind if you want, Cricket," he added, speaking to Alfie. "Without any shouting," he added.

As if he needed to say that!

Alfie looked back at EllRay just before following her dad out the door.

Help, she said—without making any noise.

Good luck, he replied silently.

Feeling Guilty

"What was all that about upstairs?" Alfie's mom asked as Alfie and her dad came into the family room. Mrs. Jakes was stitching lacy trim to the hem of the princess gown. She had been working on it all day.

"Just a small difference of opinion, it seems," her husband said, settling down on the sofa with the newspaper. "A skirmish," he added. "Probably pre-Halloween jitters."

"But everything's fine now?" Alfie's mom asked, still worried.

"It's perfect," Alfie said. "Ooh," she added, rushing over to the sofa to look at her costume. "That's so pretty, Mom. You finished it!"

"Almost. And I'm pleased with it," Alfie's mother said, smiling as she held it up for inspection.

Alfie had tried the gown on—partly finished—when she got home from school. It was made from light pink silky fabric, with flower-petal-like poofs over the shoulders and hips.

It was the most beautiful dress ever, Alfie thought.

"Which tiara are you going to wear with it?" her mom asked. "The pointy one, or the little one with the pearls?"

"I can't decide," Alfie said, snuggling in as close to her mom as she could without wrinkling the gown. "I don't want to copy anyone else's tiara, so I might bring them both to school. That way I can choose at the last minute."

"All right, if you keep them in their little boxes," Alfie's mom said as she held the hem of the gown up again to look at it. "We'll put them in the bag with your costume. I wonder what the other All-Stars are going to wear."

And just like that, Alfie was thinking again about Bella—and nice Mrs. Babcock. Mrs. Babcock had to have worked twice as hard on two bunny costumes as her own mom had worked on this one princess gown. And for what?

As for Bella, she was probably lying in bed right now, too excited to sleep. She would be imagining the fun she thought she and Alfie were going to have tomorrow.

Matching bunnies.

It *was* a cute idea, Alfie admitted to herself.

"I'm feeling guilty," Alfie announced—and then she shrank back into the sofa cushions, horrified that she'd spoken the words aloud.

Her mom had always told both Alfie and EllRay that guilt was a kind of early warning system your brain used to tell you that you were doing something wrong.

Thanks, brain, Alfie thought, making a secret face.

"Guilty about what, sweetie?" her mother asked, frowning. "Don't feel bad about asking me to make you a costume at the last minute," she said. "I mean, I wouldn't have minded a little more advance notice, I'll admit. But I really enjoyed myself today."

"Your book, though," Alfie said, going along with her mom's idea that interfering with her writing was what Alfie felt guilty about. Because— how could she explain what was about to happen? It was so complicated!

No, it's not complicated, she told herself silently in a let's-not-mess-around kind of voice. You want to be a princess instead of a bunny. It's simple.

Alfie almost groaned aloud. Should she confess and tell her mom about the bunny costume Mrs. Babcock had made for her? Tell her about Bella's excitement because she thought she would be doing something special with a new friend?

But telling her mother about the bunny costume meant telling her dad, too, Alfie reminded
herself, peeking over at her father. And he would
probably turn it into a great big lesson.

"Did you ever feel guilty about something
when you were a kid, Mom?" Alfie asked, mostly
to quiet that pesky voice inside her head.

"Me?" her mom asked, surprised. "Oh, heavens,
yes."

"Same here," Alfie's dad said from his end of
the sectional. "When I was about nine years old,
I was supposed to sell a box of giant candy bars
for a school fundraiser. And I succeeded. But
then I lost the envelope that had all the checks
and money inside."

"You did?" Alfie said, her eyes wide. "So what
happened?"

"My father ended up paying for everything,"
Dr. Jakes said. "But of course I had to pay him
back—with my allowance. It took almost the whole
school year, too," he added, shaking his head at the
memory.

"Well, my guilty secret isn't *quite* so bad," Alfie's mom said, laughing. "But when *I* was about nine, a neighbor asked my mother if she could store some very fancy cookies she'd bought in the extra freezer in our garage. They were for a special meeting," she explained. "A book club, I think. But I took a peek at them, of course, and they just looked so *good.*"

"Uh-oh," Alfie said.

"'Uh-oh' is right," her mom said, laughing. "Because I helped myself to just *one*, and you couldn't even tell it was gone. It was delicious, too—even though it was frozen when I ate it. That just made it better, in fact," she added. "Like a cookie popsicle."

"Yum," Alfie said.

"But then the next day," her mom continued, "I decided to eat another cookie or two. And when the neighbor lady came over to get her cookies the morning of her meeting, that was one mighty light cookie box, let me tell you. I had eaten *thirty-two cookies.* My poor mother didn't know what to say, or where to look. She was *mortified.*"

"That means embarrassed," Alfie's father said, interpreting.

"So your goof-up was really worse than Dad's," Alfie said, amazed. "Even though you said it wasn't. Because Dad's mistake was just one very small thing," she pointed out, echoing her own words to Bella. "And it was really just an accident. But, Mom, you decided to do something wrong over and over again. On purpose. Like a criminal!"

There, Alfie thought, satisfied. How could her mom get mad at her for a harmless fib when she had basically broken the law?

"Gee, thanks, Alfie," her mother said, laughing.

"So the lesson is, *nobody's perfect,*" Alfie said, hoping her parents would remember these two familiar words tomorrow afternoon.

"I suppose no one is," her mother agreed, thinking about it. "But they can get a lot closer to perfection than your father and I did, I hope."

Alfie took a deep breath. "I think your mother and father should have told you everything was okay, Mom," she said, hoping her parents would remember this advice tomorrow. "You suffered enough."

"But I didn't suffer at all," her mom protested,

laughing again. "I did exactly what I wanted to do every day for an entire week. And I knew what I was doing, too."

Alfie hadn't known her mom could be that bad when she was a kid! Or her dad, either. That careless, anyway. And in a way, she told herself, what her parents had done when they were kids was a lot worse than what *she* was doing.

And she was only seven years old, not nine.

"I'd better put myself to bed," she told them. "Because tomorrow—"

"Tomorrow is going to be a very big day," her mother said, finishing the sentence for her. "Goodnight, sweetie."

16

A Big Fuzzy Blur

"Whoa, Mom," Alfie said at the kitchen island on Friday morning as she tried to finish her cereal. "That bag is as big as a suitcase!"

Mrs. Jakes was at the dining room table, folding the princess gown in tissue paper for its trip to Oak Glen Primary School. Alfie tried to imagine sneaking the large, glossy bag past Bella as she walked up the school's front steps "Oh, this?" she might tell her friend. "It's nothing!"

Alfie couldn't even *think* about the part of the day when Bella would find out what she'd really be wearing to the Halloween parade and party. There was a big fuzzy blur in her brain where that future event was hiding out.

How did she ever get *in* such a mess?

"But the bag won't be heavy," her mother told Alfie from the dining room. Now she was crumpling sheets of tissue paper to stuff inside the princess gown's skirt to keep it poofy. "We don't want any wrinkles, do we?"

"No," Alfie said, wiping a dribble of milk from her chin. "Did EllRay already leave for school?" she asked.

"Mm-hmm," her mom said, nodding. "With his costume in a brown paper bag. I guess it's a *bi-i-i-g* secret," she added, laughing and looking a tiny bit worried at the same time. "Heaven only knows what those boys have planned for the parade. Listen," she continued, reaching for more paper. "I put your tiara boxes at the bottom of the bag. Oh, I wish you girls didn't have to change into your costumes in the *bathroom*," she added, shaking her head.

"I know. It's gross," Alfie said, making a face. "But they promised it would be nice and clean, for once. And Miss Myrna from the office will be there in case we need any help," she added. "The girls' room is the only place where there's enough privacy for thirteen girls to change, Mom."

"I suppose," Mrs. Jakes said. "So, let's see. You're going to eat lunch," she began, trying to get that afternoon's plan straight. "Then you'll all go to the cubby room to get your costumes, and then you'll go the the girls' room to change. Correct?"

"Mm-hmm," Alfie said, nodding.

"And then you will go *back* to the cubby room and leave your regular clothes there," her mom continued. "Then you'll all go out to the playground to line up for the parade. Do I have that right?"

Alfie bit her lip. Her poor, innocent mom had left out the part about how there would be one lonely little All-Star bunny—Bella—hopping out to the playground behind the prettiest princess posse in the world. And there would be an awesome Dragon Girl as well, and maybe a *quinceañera* pretend-teenager or two in whirly, twirly pastel dresses.

"Right," Alfie said, stirring the leftover milk in her cereal bowl.

Princess Alfie. She should be feeling good

about today, Alfie told herself—not bad, with a jangly tummy.

✳   ✳   ✳

Alfie climbed out of the Sobels' car as Mrs. Sobel popped open the trunk. "Now, you girls get some real schoolwork done this morning," Hanni's mom said, making sure Hanni and Alfie each got the right costume bag. "That way, you will have earned the fun you're going to have this afternoon."

Mrs. Sobel had such a weird way of looking at things! It was as if she thought people didn't deserve to be happy unless they were miserable first. Alfie was grateful it wasn't like that at *her* house, where her cheerful mom often said, "Celebrate the small things!" The Jakes family was always having little parties.

For an encouraging rejection letter for one of her mom's books.

For a perfect "Decimal Multiplication" quiz for EllRay.

For an entire week going by without Alfie leaving something at school.

Poor Hanni and her mom, Alfie thought, shaking her head. It seemed like they didn't have *nearly* as much fun as her family did.

Alfie hoisted her backpack onto her shoulders so she could hold the big costume bag in front of her like the treasure that it was.

"Alfie," a husky voice called from the top of the stairs.

Bella. "Hi-*eee*," Alfie said, her heart thudding.

"Hi. What's in that bag?" Bella asked, frowning a little. "I already put our costumes in the cubby room."

"This?" Alfie asked, glancing down at the bag she was holding. "It's—it's just snacks and decorations for later on. For the party. My mom asked me to bring them to school early."

The fib flew right out of her mouth!

She was getting to be just a little too good at this, Alfie told herself. Was lying something that got easier each time you did it—like cartwheels?

"I hope there's no ice cream in there," Bella joked.

Bella totally believed her. Alfie didn't know whether to laugh or cry, and there wasn't time to find out.

"No ice cream," she said.

"Well, let's put your bag in the cubby room so we can go out back and play," Bella said. "I can't believe we have to wait until after lunch to start having the *real* fun."

The two girls stowed Alfie's bag and hurried out to the playground. There was still time to enjoy some before-school excitement on this special day. Bella would be okay this afternoon, Alfie thought again—hanging out by herself.

She was *that strong*.

And if Alfie's costume made Bella a little sad, she'd get over it.

Maybe she will, and maybe she won't, Alfie told herself silently—but she was full of doubt.

In her class's Opinion Writing unit yesterday, Alfie reminded herself, they had talked about the difference between opinions and facts. And it was Alfie's *opinion* that she wanted to be a princess.

But it was a *fact* that Bella's feelings would be hurt because of it, Alfie admitted now. And that was no lie.

Okay, Alfie thought, still feeling stubborn.

So maybe Bella *wouldn't* get over the costume switch—and Alfie's near-fibbing—so fast after all. But Bella would get over being the only bunny more quickly than Alfie would get over missing out on being a princess for Halloween.

And she should put herself first, Alfie told herself in the early morning light.

Right?

One Last Battle

Alfie tried to avoid Bella the rest of the morning.

Even though Bella sat at the table behind her in class, Alfie didn't turn around once. And when Bella was chosen to pass out the "Know Your Capital Letters!" worksheets to the class during Writing Workshop, Alfie took hers in a way-too-interested manner, not looking at her friend.

At morning recess, Alfie didn't get her snack from the cubby room with the other kids, including Bella. Instead, she scampered down to the lower playground as fast as she could. And when Arletty came skipping down the path, Alfie said they should have a race around the playground, even though she knew Arletty would win.

Around and around they went, like two hamsters on a wheel, until Alfie could barely see or think straight.

"*Something About Me,*" she whispered to herself, feeling dizzy as she remembered last weekend's homework assignment. "*I am a girl who is about to hurt my friend's feelings! Exclamation mark.*"

By the time the back-to-class buzzer was about to sound, Alfie saw that Bella was deep in conversation with Phoebe and Estella. Bella looked up and smiled at Alfie. She put one hand behind her head, raising two fingers above some wayward tufts of shining, dark-gold hair.

Bunny ears.

Alfie tried to smile back.

✳   ✳   ✳

At lunch, the All-Star girls were quiet for a change, though few of them could eat. It was as if they were too busy picturing themselves in the parade.

"How are we supposed to eat lunch when we're so excited?" Lulu asked as the All-Star girls hovered around the picnic tables like restless bees.

"I don't know," Alfie said, trying to wash down a bite of her pita bread sandwich with a gulp of cold milk. She could barely swallow.

At a nearby table, the boys seemed to be managing to eat just fine.

Nothing ever bothered the boys, it seemed to Alfie.

On the playground, some office grown-ups and a few parent volunteers were setting up loudspeakers for the parade music. It had been an ordinary playground just this morning, Alfie thought, amazed. But it would be a magical place this afternoon—a place where anything might happen.

Noisy, crackling bursts of "Thriller" seemed to split the air every few seconds as Principal James fiddled with a small control panel. A bossy-looking father hovered at his side.

* * *

"Come on. Hurry," Bella urged Alfie, Phoebe, and long-haired Estella after the buzzer sounded, and the playground kids were heading for their classrooms. It was time to change for the Halloween parade!

"The boys are gonna get dressed in our classroom," Bella reminded them, "and we don't want to have to watch."

"Ew, *no*, we don't," Phoebe said, blushing at the idea.

"They'll probably all be Spider-Man for Halloween," Estella predicted as quietly as possible, given the noise in the room. "Or some Star Wars guys from that movie a couple of years ago. Because boys are just lazier about Halloween than us girls are, that's all."

Alfie wasn't so sure. Scooter, Bryan, and even shy Alan had been whooping it up more than usual all during lunch, hadn't they? Alfie thought Halloween was probably a big deal for them, too. It sure was for EllRay, and he was *old*.

"I don't care," Phoebe said, still pink. "I still believe in privacy."

"So let's hurry, you guys," Bella said, elbowing her way into the crowded cubby room. "I'll get our two bags, Alfie," she yelled over her shoulder.

And then I'll get my one bag, Alfie said to herself.

Surprise, Bella!

✳   ✳   ✳

The girls' restroom was churning with excitement as—with the help of Miss Myrna—the second-grade All-Star girls struggled out of their school clothes and into their Halloween costumes. *Oohs* and *aahs* floated like bubbles in the soap-scented air as the girls saw each others' gowns for the first time.

For once, everyone was being really nice at the same time, Alfie noticed. Even Suzette, who had first called dibs on being the class princess. Their voices mingled as they echoed in the tiled bathroom.

"So pretty!"

"Are those real diamonds?"

"What's that?" Bella asked, seeing Alfie holding her big shiny costume bag. Halfway into her fleecy pink bunny suit, Bella looked much more flustered than usual, Alfie noticed.

It *was* kind of warm in there. Or was Bella having second thoughts about being a bunny?

"Oops," Alfie said, pretending to be surprised as she looked down at her tissue-topped bag. "I guess I brought the snacks bag by mistake, I got so excited."

Okay, she scolded herself—now, she was flat-out lying to Bella.

She had been lying all along, really.

"Well, this one's for you," Bella said, scooting the second bag toward Alfie with her foot as she tried to hold her costume against her chest. "You better hurry up, Alfie, or we'll miss seeing the little kids start the parade."

"I'm gonna change in one of the stalls," Alfie told her as if she'd just gotten the idea.

"Where the *potties* are?" Bella asked, aghast. "But you'll get your costume all wet and yucky!"

"I'm not changing *in* the potty," Alfie assured her, faking a laugh. "Just next to it. Don't worry. I'll be careful," she added, dragging both bags with her into the toilet stall.

Thank goodness it was clean, as promised, Alfie thought, looking around. And the floor was dry.

Perfect for her silky pink gown.

It was Princess Alfie time!

"Hurry up, ladies," Miss Myrna sang from somewhere near the bathroom sinks. "Call out if you need any help. Zippers or buttons, anyone?"

Help, Alfie wanted to yell. *Help, help, help! Someone tell me what to do!*

She could almost hear imaginary swords clanking as Nice Alfie and Selfish Alfie battled it out inside her head—just like in a Saturday morning cartoon.

And she knew that both Alfies were her.

"Go ahead and be a princess," she imagined Selfish Alfie saying. *"You know you want to. And Mom worked so hard on your dress. You'll hurt her feelings if you come out dressed like a <u>rabbit</u>."*

"No. Be a bunny," Nice Alfie might say. *"You kind of promised Bella, really. And Mrs. Babcock worked so hard. And Mom will understand, once you tell her the whole story. You can be a princess on the <u>real</u> Halloween."*

"No!" Selfish Alfie would probably cry, stomping an invisible foot.

Selfish Alfie was like that.

"Last call, ladies," Miss Myrna called out in her best that's-that, no-nonsense tone of voice. "Hurry and line up, please." And Alfie reached deep into one of the bags.

What You Do

"Ta-da!" Alfie said, hopping out of the toilet stall in her lavender bunny costume. Her front paws were in the air, but her pointy tiara was clamped firmly to her head, just in front of her ears.

She held the other tiara in her fleecy paw.

"Ooh," the girls squealed, laughing, and a couple of them clapped. Alfie was relieved, hearing the applause. "Bella and I are the Princess Bunnies," she announced, handing the second tiara to a beaming Bella. *"Thanks, Alfie,"* Bella whispered, perching the tiara in front of her floppy pink ears.

"You guys should *for sure* hop in front of the rest of us in the parade," Hanni said, excited.

"Like, you're magic, and you're leading the way."

"It'll be good luck for everyone," Suzette announced with a very un-princess-y fist pump.

"Okay. If you insist," Alfie said, sneaking Bella a smile.

"Don't forget your bags of clothes, ladies," Miss Myrna said, counting the lined-up girls before heading off down the hall to Mr. Havens's classroom.

"Listen up," their teacher was saying as the girls traipsed through the door. They blushed and giggled as the boys stared at their costumes.

"Hi-*eee*," Hanni said, flouncing her skirts.

"*Wha-a-at?*" Scooter exclaimed, his eyes wide as he gaped at the girls' fancy costumes.

"*Oh*," Mr. Havens said, staggering to his chair and pretending to gasp at the sight of them. "All this beauty in one small room? This wonderful posse of princesses? *And* a Dragon Girl, and two princess rabbits, as well? I don't think I can stand it! But you lovely ladies had better—"

"*Stow our gear*," the girls chorused, quoting one of their teacher's familiar sayings.

Alfie felt relieved at having an ordinary chore to do. But they did look pretty good, she thought, straightening her bunny ears and fluffing her tail. Even the boys had looked impressed as they watched the girls hop or glide by, their long ears at a perky angle and their skirts swaying like silken bells.

On every princess head, and on two bunny heads, tiaras glittered.

And Dragon Girl? Arletty was usually a pretty quiet kid, in Alfie's opinion. But today, she was striking powerful poses left and right.

Even the boys were looking good today, Alfie had to admit. Scooter was a blood-dripping zombie, and Bryan was a knight in plastic armor, which should make her history-loving mom happy, Alfie thought. And shy Alan was an amazing, giant slice of pizza. He could barely sit down without a slice of pepperoni falling off.

So Estella had been wrong about the boys not caring about Halloween!

"Hup, hup," Mr. Havens said as he herded his class together. He fiddled with his collar for a second—and his tie lit up. *An electric tie!*

How cool was that? All the kids laughed and cheered.

"Off we go, All-Stars," Mr. Havens announced, organizing them all with a single wave of his hand. "And stick together!"

* * *

Outside, in the perfect October afternoon, "Monster Mash" was already booming across the playground where all seven grades were gathered, grouped by class.

Principal James—dressed as a pirate king—was leading the festivities. "Let the grand parade begin!" he shouted into a squealing microphone.

And, to the sound of "Purple People Eater," the littlest kids started walking around the playground in a wobbly line. They were shy at first, as if awed by the occasion. But they smiled once they heard the cheers.

The first-grade kids came after that, of course. And that's when Mr. Havens's All-Stars started to get nervous.

They were next.

The princesses started adjusting each other's tiaras and fluffing their own skirts.

Alfie and Bella bumped paws.

And—it was the All-Stars' turn!

"Rabbits first, then the princesses, then Dragon Girl, and then all you awesome boys,"

Mr. Havens called out as "Ghostbusters" started to play.

"Who ya gonna call?"

"Ghostbusters!" all the second-graders yelled, as if they'd rehearsed it.

Alfie looked for her mom in the audience.

Mrs. Jakes was standing next to Suzette's mom, Mrs. Monahan, Alfie saw—one hand shielding her eyes from the sun's glare as she tried to spot Alfie. And it looked like Mrs. Monahan was going to have a baby. Soon!

Excited, Suzette tapped Alfie on her fleecy shoulder. "If I have good luck all year, it will be a girl," she yelled over the music.

"That's great, Suzette," Alfie shouted back, smiling. "But brothers aren't so bad. Mom! Over here," she cried, waving her lavender bunny arm in the air to get her mother's attention. *"I'll explain later,"* she tried to yell, once she'd caught her mother's eye.

But her mom just made a gigantic shrugging gesture and laughed, shaking her head. *"Oh, for heaven's sake!"* Alfie could almost hear her say.

The All-Stars felt let down after they had completed their part in the parade. But then here came the sixth-graders, swagger-walking to the old *Addams Family* song. They couldn't have known what would be playing during their part of the parade. But they got into the spirit of the song at once, all snapping their fingers at the exact right time.

Snap, snap!

The girls, most of whom looked bigger and older than the boys, were really cute, in Alfie's opinion. But it was the boys, led by EllRay Jakes, who were creating the biggest stir—because most of them had dressed up as Coach Havens, their recess hero!

Each boy carried a basketball and wore some version of Mr. Havens's trademark skinny tie, shirt with rolled-up sleeves, and sunglasses, like the ones Mr. Havens usually wore on the playground. They had somehow also managed to capture his walk—kind of loose and cool, but athletic.

They bounced their basketballs in unison. It was awesome.

Behind her, Alfie could hear her teacher's deep roar of laughter, followed by laughs from the audience as they got the joke. They rose to their feet and applauded during this last part of the parade.

Alfie felt so proud. Way to go, EllRay!

* * *

The All-Star kids were relaxed but excited as they walked back to class—and to the Halloween party that volunteers had thrown together during the parade.

Bella had been walking behind Alfie, talking with *quinceañera*-girl Estella again. But she skipped through the crowd to catch up with her bunny-twin before they reached the open school door. "That was so much fun, Alfie," she said, a little out of breath. "Thanks for being a bunny with me. I know you didn't really want to, except at first."

Alfie's breath caught in her throat. "You *knew*?" she asked, her face turning hot.

"Kind of," Bella said. "But you did it anyway, and that was cool. My mom always says that it's what you do that counts," she added, giving Alfie a friendly nudge.

She *had* done the right thing, Alfie told herself—by being loyal to her friend.

This time.

But Alfie had the sudden feeling that the war to figure out the right thing to do was something you had to keep fighting time after time.

Battle after battle.

That sounded hard, she thought silently.

"Like you said, it was fun," Alfie told Bella. "Absolutely."

"And the party's gonna be fun, too," Bella said with a grin. "Race you to the door?"

"Why not?" Alfie said, laughing. "I'm feeling lucky!"

And off they went—ready for the best time ever.

Keep an eye out for other
ABSOLUTELY
Alfie
stories!